Digital Disaster

HyperLinkz

Digital Disaster

BOOK **1** ROBERT ELMER

WaterBrook
P R E S S

DIGITAL DISASTER
PUBLISHED BY WATERBROOK PRESS
2375 Telstar Drive, Suite 160
Colorado Springs, Colorado 80920
A division of Random House, Inc.

Unless noted in *The Hyperlinkz Guide to Safe Surfing,* all Web-site names are fabrications of the author.

ISBN 1-57856-747-5

Published in association with the literary agency of Alive Communications, Inc., 7680 Goddard Street, Suite 200, Colorado Springs, CO 80920.

Library of Congress Cataloging-in-Publication Data
Elmer, Robert.
    Digital disaster / Robert Elmer.—1st ed.
       p. cm.—(HyperLinkz ; #1)
    Summary : When twelve-year-olds Austin and Ashley Webster are accidentally scanned into the Internet, they must follow the most unlikely links to survive, and to make it back home.
    ISBN 1-57856-747-5
    1. Internet—Fiction. 2. Christian life—Fiction. 3. Science fiction. I. Title.
PZ7.E4794Dg 2004
[Fic]—dc22   2003025420

Printed in the United States of America
2004—First Edition

10 9 8 7 6 5 4 3 2

Contents

CHAPTER 1

Doggie Data Dump

"Please, please, *please* tell me you didn't pay thirteen dollars for that piece of junk."

Ashley Webster didn't want to say, "I told you so." But the thought crossed her mind that if her older brother, Austin, spent half as much time on his homework as he did at garage sales or taking pictures of birds, he'd get straight A's, no problem. She wasn't going to bring it up one more time, but if Mom found out how he had spent his birthday bucks from Grandma Wallis...

"I told you it's not a piece of junk," Austin finally said a few seconds after his sister thought he would answer. The pause was like the time between a flash of lightning and one thousand one, one thousand two, one thousand three, and—*bam!*—the thunder rumbles. But that was just Austin, and it wasn't because he was missing any smarts.

Actually, talking to Austin sometimes reminded Ashley of

watching a TV reporter live in China or any other place far from the university town of Normal, Illinois, where Ashley and Austin lived with their mom and dad on Fell Avenue in a nice, old, white house with two gable windows. The news lady here asks a question, and the overseas reporter just waits there for a few seconds while the message bounces off a satellite. Finally, the reporter hears the question and nods.

Just like Austin.

"It's a real digital camera," he told Ashley, "and it's going to work perfectly if you'll just hold the dog still."

The camera actually looked like a regular old snapshot camera, silver and scratched and perched on a three-legged tripod that made it look like a weird stork standing right there in their garage. Austin had wired it directly to his beat-up laptop so they could use the snapshots for the Web site they were creating. He'd set up the laptop on their dad's workbench, which didn't have much else on it. The Websters' dad was a doctor at the Normal Community Hospital—definitely not Mr. Fix-It.

"I hope Applet appreciates all the work we're doing to put together her Web site." Ashley sighed and scratched her freckled nose with her free hand. "It's not every dog—"

"Yeah, I've got it. Hold it right there."

Ashley ducked down so that she wouldn't get her hand in the picture of their aunt Jessica Mulligan's purebred, grand-champion beagle. Applet was cute and worth tons of money, but that wasn't stopping her from getting a little antsy sitting on a tippy folding card table under hot lights.

Ashley felt just as antsy. Applet licked her hand as if to make her feel better. Oh, she was a really fine dog—if you didn't count the digging and the nighttime howling. That, and the fact that every time the door opened—*whoosh*—Applet was gone. It had happened the first time Ashley dog-sat last year when Aunt Jessica and her family went on vacation for a week. Other than that, sure, Applet was a great dog. Oh, and she was due to have champion puppies sometime soon.

"Ma-a-an." Austin shook his head and fiddled with the connections one more time. Ashley had to admit that if anybody at Chiddix Junior High could make a garage-sale camera come to life, it would be her brother.

"Everything looks like it's working," he mumbled. "I just can't get it to…"

FLASH!

"Whoa!" Ashley nearly fell over backward, but the stars wouldn't be going away anytime soon. Red ones, yellow ones…

"Yes! There it goes. Now let's try it again."

Ashley rubbed her eyes and turned back to the card table, but the flash must have scared Applet, too, and she must have hopped down.

"Applet?" Ashley peeked under the table. She didn't blame

the pooch. This photo session was getting out of hand. "Come on back, girl. Just one more."

"Did you see where she went?" Austin got down on his hands and knees next to the workbench. No Applet. "I didn't even hear her jump off the table."

"Well, she couldn't have gone far." Ashley looked around the garage. A ray of summer sunshine poked in through a single window. "Here, girl."

Before it got too terribly hot—the way it always did in July—this wasn't such a bad place to hang out. Like a lot of garages in Normal, it had been built as a carriage house when more people owned horses than cars. That meant it was smaller than Ashley's friend Amy's big, two-car garage over in the newer part of town. That meant it held only one small car, Sven, her dad's trusty, old gray Volvo. And that meant that besides hiding underneath Sven or behind Austin's drum set, there really wasn't anywhere else for Applet to hide.

"This is too weird." Austin lifted himself off the floor and clapped the dust from his hands. Compared to most kids his age, he had a little more of himself to lift.

"She's really not under there?" Ashley checked for herself. No Applet—just the usual puddle of oil. The fold-up garage door that opened out onto Fell Avenue was closed tight. So was the door to the backyard. Ashley rattled the doorknob to make sure.

"Wait a minute." When Austin sounded like he had another one of his great ideas, Ashley got ready to groan. "I've seen something like this before."

"Yeah?" Ashley checked once more behind Sven's back tires just to be extra, extra sure, then she peeked behind the easel where her brother's latest bird painting sat. No luck.

"It was on the *Amazing Crispin the Magician Show*. He had this lady on a table, and they covered her with a blanket. Then there was a big flash of light and—"

And that's when their aunt Jessica stepped in from the backyard, as if to say, Ta-da! Dramatic, the way she always stepped into a room. She tossed her long blond hair like one of those girls in a shampoo commercial and looked around the garage. But here's the thing about Aunt Jessica: Like Ashley, she was just twelve, the late-edition baby who surprised Grandma Wallis and Grandpa Reuben with her arrival. Well, maybe *surprised* isn't the best word. *Floored* or *shocked* might be better—as in she blew them away. So, yes, Jessi was Austin and Ashley's aunt because she was their mom's much, much younger sister. She was also the very proud owner of a national-champion beagle, with a room full of blue ribbons and trophies to prove it.

Make that a *missing* national-champion beagle. As in gone. Disappeared. AWOL. (That means Absent Without Official Leave, for those who aren't in the military.)

"Hey, guys." She checked out the garage, the camera, the lights, and the table. She was probably wondering when it would be her turn to smile for the camera. "How's the photo shoot coming? Where's Applet?"

Ashley gulped. What was she going to say? We lost your five-thousand-dollar show dog? One minute she was here, and the next minute, *poof?*

"I think we got the digital camera working." Austin looked like he was sweating, though it was not quite hot enough for that yet.

"That's right," agreed Ashley. She felt sweat trickle down her own forehead when she heard a faint dog whimper.

But unless she was going crazy, the sound wasn't coming from behind the drum set, and it wasn't coming from under the car either.

"Woof." There it was again! She bent closer to the workbench when she heard the bark.

It was coming from the speakers of Austin's laptop.

CHAPTER 2

CyberGLaciers

"Oh, so you *did* take the pictures already." Jessi bent over the laptop display to ooh and aah. "That was quick. And these are totally cute. With sound effects and everything."

Sound effects? Ashley heard the dog whimpering through the stereo speakers too. But Austin was busy clicking around the Web site with a look on his face that said, "I don't get it."

Well, neither did Ashley.

Oh, she understood technical stuff—maybe not as well as her brother, but enough to make a computer work. He had some kind of wireless card installed in his laptop that meant he could surf the Internet without being plugged into the cable connection in the house. And before they'd started taking pictures of Applet, he'd been checking out a Web site about the wreck of the *Titanic*. It was still up on his screen, but now...

"I like that shot." Jessi pointed at a black-and-white photo of a person waving from the deck of the huge ship as it was leaving port. A black-and-white beagle looked over the railing too. "How did you manage to make it look so real? It's as if Applet's right there."

"As if." Austin scratched his head and clicked on another photo, this one of a beagle sitting by the ship's big steering wheel, her paws on the spokes. Another showed a beagle perched next to a table centerpiece in the ship's ballroom. Applet looked as if she was getting around. And in every shot she was wearing her same cute beagle smile.

"Applet on the *Titanic*. Show me how you did it," Jessi insisted.

Austin just shook his head. "All I got was one flash, and I wasn't even sure that one worked."

"Oh, come on. You can show me."

Jessi wasn't giving up, so Austin shrugged his shoulders and fiddled with the camera once more. He turned it around to face his sister.

"Okay, if you really want to know, it's pretty simple. All I do is point and shoot. The shots download here. Then I touch up the photos, and we drop them onto the Web site. See?"

It was demo time. He pointed the camera at Ashley.

"Look, I'll do a sample for you. Smile, Ashley." Maybe Austin was thinking that if he goofed around long enough, Applet would come back or Jessi would grow bored and leave. Either way, when the flash went off, Ashley was seeing stars.

Only this time her ears buzzed almost as if she were listening to an out-of-tune radio station. Her hands shook and her short-cut auburn hair felt as if it were standing on end, a Frankenstein experiment.

"Austin, you've got to shut off that flash next time."

What was wrong with that silly camera anyway? Ashley shivered, partly from an electric tingle, partly from the freezer-blast of cold that suddenly hit her as she popped out of an Amazing Crispin the Magician–style cloud of fog.

One look told her this was definitely not normal. Not Normal either. *Yikes!*

"Austin?" she whispered. What had happened to their nice, comfy garage on Fell Avenue?

A gray wood deck throbbed beneath her feet as if it were alive. Ashley gripped a damp metal railing for balance, but then yanked her hand back at the shock of its slick, icy-cold feel. It felt too much like a frozen dead fish.

She hugged herself to get warm, but she could tell her nose was about to freeze solid. Not that Ashley hadn't lived through plenty of cold winters in Normal, but—*sniff*—wasn't this supposed to be July?

"Jessi?"

Off in the inky black night, Ashley could make out ghostly white shadows like mountains of ice. Glaciers. Water hissed by below. The ship she now stood on—if that's what it was—

glittered and sparkled with lights, a floating, humming carnival. To prove it, a brass band of some kind played in the distance, and a few stray notes drifted her way. Beethoven?

"I have a feeling we're not in Kansas anymore, Toto," she whispered, but there wasn't a little dog anywhere in sight. Not even the Great Oz. Instead, a couple about her parents' age strolled by, all dressed up in furs and long wool coats as if they were going to the opera. *They look*—Ashley couldn't quite put her finger on it—*different*. But the way they looked at her... Hadn't they ever seen a shivering girl in jeans and an orange Chiddix Chargers T-shirt?

Only now it wasn't orange the way it had been back in Normal; it was a medium gray like so much else she saw. Everything was black and white and gray with not a spot of color to warm the picture.

"Nice outside tonight, huh?" Ashley asked them. If there was one thing she was good at, it was landing on her feet. And if she was going crazy, she would go crazy in style.

But the couple changed direction, as if they'd decided, "This is a very strange person, and we're going to pretend we didn't see her." The woman leaned over and said something to the man as they kept walking. It sounded like, "She's an internaut, dear."

Even if this was a wild dream, Ashley decided she'd better get inside before she froze to death. She started to wrestle open a brass-handled door just as an officer in a trim black uniform sprinted around the corner, booming like a foghorn.

"Hold the hatch closed!" he shouted, waving and pointing at the deck. "The beagle!"

CHAPTER 3

Left Behind?

"I didn't just do that, did I?" Back in the family garage, Austin looked hard at where his sister had been standing seconds ago. Maybe his glasses had stopped working.

Jessica's mouth hung as wide open as her nephew's.

"Awesome."

Awesome wasn't exactly the word Austin would have used. And this time he knew it wouldn't do any good to look beneath Sven.

Ashley was gone.

Gone, as in departed, removed, vanished, missing. As in…major uh-oh.

"You don't think…" Jessi's eyes grew big as if she'd just thought of the same thing Austin had. She went to the same youth group, after all, and she'd read the same best-selling thriller novels. Everybody in the youth group had read them. They were all about the Rapture, when all the true Christians are supposed to be taken up to heaven, and everybody else is, well...

"No way." But Austin ran to the doorway with her, and they both stared out at the street to see who else had been left behind. He pinched himself. Why would *he* still be here? This was not the way the story was supposed to go!

"Wouldn't there be planes and cars crashing and stuff?" Jessi asked. They listened, but all Austin heard was Jessi's panicked breathing that sounded like her asthma was acting up. That and Mrs. Miller's yapping poodle next door. There sure wasn't much traffic on Fell Avenue for a Saturday morning in July.

"That's what happened in the book," Austin answered at last.

"I never actually read the book. I saw the movie, though. Kirk Cameron is *so* cute."

"He's married, Jessica. You're not supposed to say married guys are cute."

"I didn't mean anything by it. I just thought—"

"Look!" Austin pointed across the street as someone came around the side of a blue, two-story Victorian house. Mr. Hudson, pushing a mower. Mr. Hudson smiled and waved when he saw them.

"Okay, I see him, but there was a pastor who was left behind in the first book too," countered Jessi. "Wasn't there?"

Mr. Hudson was a deacon at the Normal Bible Church.

"Yeah, but Mr. Hudson is a nice guy. I really don't think he'd be left behind." Austin waved back at Mr. Hudson and turned back inside. "And I don't think *I* would be left behind either. Now *you,* I'm not so sure about."

"Stop being silly, Austin. You're creeping me out."

"That's just it. This whole thing is silly. Whacko. Like something out of the *Amazing Crispin the Magician Show* when he makes Mount Rushmore disappear."

"I saw that one too. Wasn't that cool where he—"

"Jessi, stay focused here. Ashley is *gone!* We have to do something fast."

"Other than panic, you mean? I do that really well."

He frowned at her.

"Call 911?" she tried again.

Austin closed his eyes and leaned his head back, trying to think.

"Okay," he told her, "so what happened wasn't supernatural, all right?"

"If you say so."

"It's got to be something to do with the camera. Remember the computer."

He nodded at the laptop, which still showed the Web site with the faded, old, black-and-white *Titanic* photos. Only this time, instead of all the cute beagle shots, they saw several people piled up on the deck like a football pileup after a tackle.

Strange. Austin didn't think anybody would have played foot-ball on the *Titanic*.

The screen blinked for a second, and he thought he saw something.

"There!"

They both stared at a photo of a dressed-up couple strolling the deck of the big luxury liner. Near them was a girl wearing a Chiddix Chargers T-shirt and looking pretty chilly.

Ashley.

Well, Austin knew CPR. And his doctor dad had taught him the Heimlich maneuver to help someone who is choking. He knew what he had to do.

"She's my little sister. I need to go after her."

"How?"

He pointed at the laptop's screen.

"You have to take my picture with the digital camera," he told his aunt.

"And you think you'll disappear just like Ash?" She made a sucking noise like an actress testing her breath in a mint com-mercial. "Cool."

"This is serious, Jessi. I don't know exactly where the cam-era will take me or if it'll put me in the same place as Applet and Ashley."

"Applet?" She grabbed Austin by the shoulders. "Wait a minute! Nobody said anything about Applet."

"You didn't ask."

"Oh man." Jessi crossed her arms and started to pace. "This really is serious. The dog show—"

"*Now* you're worried."

"I was worried before."

Austin swung the camera around and adjusted the focus. "Okay, well, you're going to have to help me then. Just make sure I'm totally in the frame."

She squinted at him.

"I mean," he explained, "make sure you can see all of me in the viewfinder before you hit the shutter."

"Right." She bent down and looked into the camera. "What's that red blinking light?"

"Uh-oh." He stepped over to double-check it. "I don't think I have any other batteries for this. We'd better hurry."

His aunt bobbed her head up and down. "Don't worry," she told him. "It'll be just like when those kids walked through the closet and came out to a light pole and snow."

"You mean like the wardrobe to Narnia? I didn't know you read those books."

"I saw the movie. Their English accents were *so* cute."

Austin groaned. "Just take the picture, would you?"

"Where do I press?"

"That button there." He pointed. She pressed. The camera beeped.

"Isn't it supposed to flash?"

Austin hit his forehead. *Not enough battery?*

"Press it again," he said.

"Austin, I just thought of something." She paused and blew her blond bangs out of her eyes. With all this messing around, Austin could have run to the bathroom and been back by now.

"What?"

"How are you going to get back? Have you thought of that?"

"I'll figure out something if I get there. Just press the button, will you? Please!"

"Which one again? This one?"

He reached out to point a second time when the flash went off in his face, brightly enough to knock him over backward. Austin wasn't sure which was worse, the nasty electrical shock he felt or knocking his head on the slick wood deck.

He would have grunted if the wind hadn't been knocked out of him. Instead, he pumped his legs and gasped. So this was how the fish had felt when he had pulled them into the bottom of Grandpa Reuben's boat last summer at Lake Winnebago. They had flapped their gills for a minute or two before Ashley made him throw them back.

Yeah, Austin felt just like those fish. Except this was no Lake Winnebago, and this was no fishing boat.

At least one thing about this cold, dark place was familiar. Ashley's clear-as-a-bell voice only a few feet away.

"No, I mean the *town* of Normal, in the state of Illinois! You know, the one between Iowa and Indiana."

That would be his sister, all right, the one holding a geography lesson. The person who answered her had an English accent, the kind Jessi thought was *so* cute.

"Yes, of course it is. I may be digital, but I am somewhat familiar with North American cartography. But when you said you need to get back to normal, I simply assumed—"

"This has to be a bad dream. Last I knew, my brother, Austin, and I were looking for my aunt Jessica's dog, Applet, and Austin took a picture of me with his silly digital camera, which I am going to break into a million pieces when I get home. And now…now I really have to get back to Normal."

"Hey!" Austin tried to call out, but he could still manage only a wheeze. "Over here!"

CHAPTER 4

ALice iN CyberLaND

"Terribly sorry to run you over." A man with a moustache helped Ashley to her feet. He looked real enough—two eyes, two ears, a nose, and a mouth. He even wore a black felt hat tipped to one side. A closer look revealed he was just a teensy bit out of focus, though. The skin on his hand felt more like strong static than real skin, and she was glad to let go. "I was just trying to capture the intruder. There are no dogs in this site's programming."

The programming?

"Yeah." Ashley brushed herself off. "I guess I'm not in the programming either."

"Yes, your resolution is quite good. Crystal clear. You're an internaut, aren't you?"

Ashley had to think about that one for a minute.

"I'm Ashley Webster. I don't know what an internaut is."

"Oh, the Webmaster! I've been meaning to speak with

you. There's a dead link on the home page that requires your immediate attention. Please come with me."

He started for the door, but she held back.

"No, you don't understand," Ashley replied. "My name is *Webster*, not Web *master*. And I don't know where I am."

He gave her a sideways glance as if trying to decide how crazy she was.

"Why, you're visiting *www-dot-titanic-online-dot-com*, of course, with room on board for more than twenty-five hundred virtual passengers bound for New York. Once more on our maiden voyage."

Ashley shivered. "You've done this more than once?"

He nodded. "In a digital manner of speaking. The counter says we're on episode 200,516."

"So I haven't gone back in time, then."

The man looked at her and started chuckling. Finally he threw back his head and roared.

"That's very good," he said, wiping the tears from his eyes. "Indeed. Back in time? Nothing here on the Internet is back in time. It's all *now,* my dear. Real time. Forever April 14, 1912. No future. No past."

Ashley nearly choked. Did he say 1912?

"You've clearly been reading too many fantasies," he continued. "*Alice in Wonderland,* perhaps?"

"The book with the rabbit who's always late?"

"The same." Again he chuckled as he pulled out a pocket watch on a gold chain. "And speaking of late, 11:38 is certainly past that. A Webmaster like you should be home and safely in bed."

How could she make this man understand?

"Please, I don't have the foggiest idea how to get home. All I know is my brother, Austin, took a picture of me, I felt this horrible tingling, and here I am on the deck of this ship, feeling like *Alice in Cyberland.* I sure can't stay here. Do you even know what's about to happen?"

The smile dissolved from the man's face. "If you know what's going to happen, you *are* a programmer," he told her. "Just like the woman internaut who's been lurking about."

"I'm sorry, sir." Ashley held up her hands in surrender. "I don't know who you're talking about. I hardly know anything about computers, and you've gotta believe that I'm here by mistake. I'd better just find my aunt's dog and get out of here before...before something bad happens."

Too late. An alarm bell clanged above their heads, and they heard running feet and shouts on the upper deck.

The man tipped his hat. "After this is over," he said, "perhaps you'll look into that dead link?"

"Sure." She shrugged and wondered what a real person was supposed to do on a digital *Titanic.* The cold felt cold. The water felt wet. And the hand tugging on her ankle felt clammy.

Yikes! Forget icebergs. Ashley tried to jerk her foot back and dance away, but the hand wasn't letting go.

"Ashley!"

She looked down to see someone who looked exactly like her brother clamped on to her ankle like a hungry croc. Only this was probably a virtual copy of Austin, not the real thing— just like the man she had talked to. She kicked and danced some more. For someone who wasn't real, he was holding on pretty well.

"Would you stop it?" Even his voice sounded like Austin's, but it was kind of raspy and soft, like a recording. Nice try, but nobody was going to fool her. At last she kicked him loose, and he crumpled into an outside wall.

She bent down to inspect the digital copy of her brother. He actually looked quite clear and sharp, so he was a pretty good copy, except that his left hand was almost totally see-through, as if made of ice. That was sort of creepy, to tell the truth. But the rest of him...

"Austin?" she whispered.

He groaned and looked up at her.

"That's the last time I'm going to come rescue you," he croaked.

"Is it really you?"

"Of course it's really me. I just had a rough landing, I

guess. Had to catch my breath. I was right over there while you were talking to that British guy."

"But your hand." She pointed and he whistled when he saw it.

"Whoa. I guess when the flash went off, it was out of the picture. Hope I didn't leave it back in Normal."

He wiggled his icelike fingers up close to his face, scratched his nose, shook his hand. Even though it was see-through, at least the fingers still worked.

"Yeah, well, speaking of Normal," Ashley said, "that's where we need to go. Do you know where we are? This is the—"

"The *Titanic*. I know, and it's probably sinking. You see where Applet went?"

She helped Austin up and practically dragged him across the deck.

"In here."

Meanwhile, back in Normal, Jessi tapped on the Back button on Austin's laptop, trying to pull up a picture of the *Titanic* that would show someone she recognized. No luck.

"Come out, come out, wherever you are…" she mumbled

under her breath. But all she was seeing were black-and-white photos of people in old-fashioned clothes. What happened to the ones they'd seen before?

No Austin.

No Ashley.

And no Applet.

"Come on, you guys!" She tried rapping on the square trackpad in front of the keyboard. The pointer arrow flew all over the screen, but that was all. "This isn't funny anymore."

Jessi got up and paced in front of the workbench, pulling at her ears. Sometimes that helped.

"Think! Think!" She closed her eyes, imagining what she would tell Austin and Ashley's mom.

"Don't worry," she would tell her sister. "They should be back in time for dinner. They just went for a walk on the Internet with Applet."

She groaned and ran her hands through her hair. Austin had been right about one thing. This was whacko. Totally nuts. Like something out of a movie. Time for Austin to show up from his hiding place under the Volvo and laugh at her for believing it all.

Yeah, that was it. Austin had it all planned.

If that was true, though, where was he? She began pacing again, but in her pacing she didn't notice the extension cord or how it caught on the toe of her Nike. Whoops! She nearly sprawled on the floor.

At least Jessi hadn't pulled the laptop onto the floor. At least it was—

"Uh-oh."

She fumbled with the cord and tried to plug the computer back in, but it was too late. The battery was probably already dead, and now so was the screen. Dead. Blank. Powered down.

Worse than that, if Austin and Ashley and Applet were still in there somewhere, that meant...what?

CHAPTER 5

Dot-Bomb

"I don't think Web time is the same as real time," Austin announced as they stood in the corner of a grand ballroom with a crystal chandelier and fancy dining tables piled with sliced meats and cheeses. The ship lurched and everyone in the room screamed—everyone but Austin and Ashley, that is.

"See?" Austin shook his head in amazement. "It's been, what, five minutes since we ran into the iceberg? And already the ship is sinking."

"I thought that's what it did in real life." Ashley didn't seem to see his point.

"But in real life it took two hours and forty minutes to sink."

"How do you know that?"

Austin frowned. Did his sister have to ask the captain of the Chiddix Junior High Knowledge Bowl team?

"Okay, okay." She parked her hands on her hips. "Just tell me how we're going to get off this thing."

"Let me think for a minute."

"Sounds like we don't have much more than that."

"I know. It's happening fast, like a QuickTime movie or something. Maybe we should try to find a link to somewhere else."

"But I thought this was just a Web site. You think if this ship sinks, we'll really go with it?"

"What do you think?"

Austin looked around once more. His nose puckered at the liquid dribbling from the smashed champagne bottle onto the floor. *Ack.* He could hear people shouting on deck. They sounded real enough. And he could feel the cold air blasting in from the open doors, the floor pitching beneath his feet. It all seemed real enough that he didn't want to stick around to test his guess.

"Okay," Ashley agreed, "you tell me what a link looks like, and maybe we can find one. We can ask."

They tried, but passengers wearing bulky life vests were racing by like ants. Many still had on their nightgowns underneath their vests, and no one would even stop as they scurried toward the lifeboats on deck. Yet through the mayhem, a small, eight-piece band played song after song. Finally they played one Austin recognized, a nice old hymn called "Nearer, My God, to Thee."

The ship was tilting more and more to one side, but Austin noticed one woman in the corner of the ballroom who didn't seem in a hurry to go anywhere. She stood off to the side, studying the band and drawing on a small sketch pad. She looked a lot like a teacher Ashley had once had, with long, straight black hair and a 1960s-style purple and pink blouse with a round, flowery design. It was a cool shirt, but nothing like what anyone else on the ship was wearing.

Stranger still, she looked sharp. Not sharp as in nice looking, but sharp as in not blurry.

"I think that's our link," Austin whispered in his sister's ear as they moved through the crowd toward her. Well, they *tried* to move. But every time the floor shifted, it was like trying to walk through a goofy house of mirrors at the McLean County Fair.

As they got closer to the woman, Austin noticed a slight green glow from her writing pad.

Not a pad, he thought. *A Personal Data Assistant!*

Or something like it. From ten feet away he could tell it was some kind of handheld tablet computer with a tiny keyboard at the bottom.

"Hey!" Austin tried to yell at the woman. She had to be their ticket off the sinking ship. But with all the screaming and the music and the creaking of the doomed boat, she didn't seem to hear him.

That's when things got really strange. When the woman pressed a button on her PDA, the musicians suddenly stopped cold. Another button, and they all started playing backward, as if they were undoing "Nearer, My God, to Thee."

Very weird. Austin and Ashley could only stare as the woman grinned and pressed more buttons. It was almost as if she were playing a video game and winning.

When the band reached the beginning of the hymn, they started over. Only this time it wasn't "Nearer, My God, to Thee," but a jazzy dance tune.

And the mystery woman wasn't waiting around to listen to it.

"Hey, wait a minute!" Austin broke through the crowd at last. But the woman had already turned and started to fade like the Cheshire Cat in *Alice in Wonderland*.

Curiouser and curiouser.

"Please wait!" Austin made the mistake of trying to touch the woman.

"Ow!" He quickly wrenched his hand back when it began to tingle with that peculiar, awful feeling he'd felt after the digital snapshot. By now the woman had turned almost as see-through as the fingers on his left hand. At the last moment she turned to face them before blinking completely out of sight.

"Holy cow." Ashley caught up to her brother. "Do you think she—?"

"She saw us, all right." Austin was sure of it. But before he could think about what that might mean, a dog started barking at a big plate of sliced roast beef and bread that had just slid off a table and clattered to the floor.

"Applet!" Ashley and Austin dived to grab the beagle. Ashley managed to grab a nice slice of roast beef instead. As the ship lurched, they could only watch as poor Applet scrambled for footing on the polished tile floor, slid sideways across a patch of faint blue lettering...and then faded, exactly like the woman had.

"That's it!" Austin hung sideways onto a heavy red curtain. "The link!"

He adjusted his glasses the way he always did when he had to read something close up. He practically swept the floor with his nose, but the ship swung the wrong way for him to get a good look. Ashley slid closer, hanging on to her own curtain.

"What's it say?" he yelled over the dance music.

"F-a-m—" she read, but that didn't make much sense at all.

"You're missing something," Austin told her.

"Us!"

"What?"

"Us. As in *famous*."

"Famous what?"

The ship lurched again, and Ashley's curtain started to rip.

"Famous S-h-i-p-w-r-e-c-k-s."

That did it for the curtain. Ashley swept across the floor toward the link and flickered before disappearing.

Just like the mystery woman. And Applet.

What choice did Austin have?

"Here goes."

Austin took a deep breath before he pushed off a railing and followed his sister.

Double-Clicked

"This is not real. This is not real." Ashley hoped that repeating the words enough would make it so. Kind of like Dorothy in *The Wizard of Oz* repeating, "There's no place like home. There's no place like home."

Well, if Dorothy could do it, so could she. At least this time the odd tingling feeling hadn't felt quite as creepy. Maybe she was getting used to it.

Or maybe she had slipped through the link to *Famous Shipwrecks* more easily than Austin had. Speaking of her brother, she heard a muffled yell, then "Get me outta here!"

It was pretty tough to understand him through the mound of sand. But she recognized Austin's worn running shoes pedaling in the air. Poor guy.

"Hang on!" She dropped to her knees in the warm, sugar-white sand and began digging like a dog. "I'll get you out."

Where's Applet when we need her? No matter where the dog was, Ashley couldn't leave her brother plugged headfirst in a tropical beach. After a minute or two of panic, she gave his arm a mighty tug and rolled him out onto the warm sand.

"*Pfft! Pfoo!*" Austin shook his head. "Bad landing, but thanks."

"Maybe we should stick closer together next time." Now that she was sure Austin was okay, Ashley looked around to see where the *Famous Shipwrecks* link had taken them.

Well, there was the famous shipwreck—a white, wooden yacht about the size of a fishing boat that had washed up on the beach and had a hole in its side big enough to walk through. The SS *Minnow.*

"Does this look familiar to you?" Austin stepped beneath a palm tree and fingered the leaves of a tropical bush.

"Not really. It's just a desert island with a busted boat."

Austin brought the leaf to his nose. "I thought so. Plastic."

"What's that awful music?" Ashley heard chirpy-sounding voices singing a syrupy tune, not coming from anywhere in particular, but from everywhere in general. Something about sitting back and hearing a tale about a "fateful" trip.

"Tell me we're not stuck on *Gilligan's Island,*" Ashley groaned. This was supposed to be the Internet, after all, not the home of her least favorite 1960s TV sitcom. Some famous shipwreck!

Bam! A pleasantly round, older man with bulldog cheeks stepped out from behind the plastic palm tree, straightened his red bow tie, and dusted off his pressed, black tuxedo trousers. Ashley would have run the other way, but he had the same fuzzy, out-of-focus look as the people on the *Titanic.*

"Pardon the interruption," he told them in a distinctive British accent that Jessi would have loved. "But I heard a FAQ, and it is my job to respond."

A FAQ?

"That stands for Frequently Asked Question," Austin whispered to her.

"Which FAQ did we ask?" Ashley wasn't sure she wanted to know.

"You asked where you are," announced the man. "And the answer is *www-dot-FamousShipwrecks-dot-com*—the *Gilligan's Island* page."

"Oh. So how do we get to the other famous shipwrecks?"

Almost before the words were out of her mouth, Mr. FAQ unexpectedly disappeared, and a white computer icon of a gloved hand dropped down from overhead and hit the nearby sand with a loud click. The music started up once more.

"So join us here each week my friends, you're sure to get a smile..."

Ashley tried to plug her ears as she got down on her knees. Sure enough, she could make out the words *click here to listen to the theme song* showing through the sand. This was a bad place to stand.

Click.

"Ow!" Ashley jumped and rubbed the back of her head. "What was that?"

But the clicking had just begun. Another hand pointed at Austin's shoulder, then his ear, and then there was another loud *click!*

"Hey, that hurts!" When Austin tried to duck, the hand followed, jabbing him in the back. He tried jogging down the short beach, swatting at the hand as if it were a pesky mosquito.

Click! The hand would not give up.

"Tell them to stop!" Austin spun and ducked. "I'm not Gilligan. I don't have anything to say."

True. If you clicked on a link, you went to the link. Click on a picture of Gilligan, find out more about the character. Click on Austin Webster...

Nothing.

"I think somebody's confused." When Ashley looked up, she could barely make out a large set of billboard-sized glasses peering at them from out over the ocean. Now she knew what it felt like to be a bug under a microscope.

"Hey, you!" She waved her arms and jumped up and

down. "Over here. Quit double-clicking my brother! We're not part of this site. We're just visiting."

Or just trapped.

For a moment the music stopped, and Austin lay on the sand, catching his breath.

"Now, Austin!" yelled Ashley. She waved for him to come back. He beat a quick retreat behind one of the plastic orchid plants next to a fresh set of dog footprints.

Which was fine, except that the King Kong–sized eyes squinted, and a finger tapped on something—probably the screen—in the distance. *Plink! Plink!* If Ashley had been sitting in a theater and this person had been on the movie screen, they would have been about the same size.

"Yeah, I'm talking to you!" She tried again. Could the person hear?

The face moved closer; two eyes blinked. And *click!* The hand icon came flying right at her forehead.

"Sheesh!" Ashley hit the sand facedown under a hail of double-clicks. If this were a video game, she and her brother would have been the targets. But she had more important things to worry about. And she couldn't help noticing the trail that led past Austin's hiding place.

"Did you see those paw prints?" she asked her brother after she rolled in behind him.

"I think they end right over there." He pointed to a clearing about ten feet away. Another link? Double-clicks still clattered around them on either side of the plastic shrubs. Obviously their friend in the outside world wasn't giving up so easily.

"Finding that silly dog is harder than I thought it was going to be," Ashley whispered, but she had an idea. "Tell you what. I'll stand up and count down from five. You run for the link. I'll be right behind you."

At first Austin scrunched up his face as if he wasn't too sure. But did he have a better idea? Before he could say no, Ashley stood up, stepped out from behind the bushes, and waved, "Yoo-hoo!"

Click-click! "Ouch!"

Five, four, three…

Do I really look like I'm part of an old TV show? she asked herself.

Two, one…

When Ashley turned to follow, Austin had already disappeared. But where exactly? She looked down at the sand and tried to pick out her brother's footprints from Applet's paw prints. The link had to be pretty close. She dusted off a bare spot in the sand and saw the faint glow from the lettering beneath. What did this one say?

More Famous Ships and Shipwrecks...

That's when the hand icon flew in over her shoulder, clicking on the spot before she could finish clearing off the sand.

"Uh-oh..."

Once more a tingling feeling told Ashley that she was on her way.

CHAPTER 7

Just the FAQs, Ma'am

Am I back at *www.titanic-online.com*? Ashley wondered.

She felt the same distant thrumming under her feet, the same gentle roll of a ship at sea. And at first she thought the hallway might have been on the massive ocean liner, though it was obviously not nearly as grand as any she'd seen earlier. What had happened to the fancy wood paneling?

"Are you here for a tour of our two ships, the *Doulos* and the *Logos*?" asked a girl.

Ashley turned to see a group of smiling college students.

"Not exactly." What had happened to the *More Famous Ships and Shipwrecks* link? This wasn't a shipwreck.

At least not yet.

She tried to explain. "I need to find—"

"In English, Spanish, German, Danish, French, or Chinese?" asked another student.

"English, I guess, but—"

That was enough for the six Web guides. The first one, a dark-haired guy who looked as if he might have been from Latin America, stepped to the front.

"Welcome to *www-dot-ourships-dot-d-e*," he began. He must have done this before. "Our ships have been serving the nations since 1970. The vessels have visited ports in over 135 countries in the Americas, Africa, Europe, Asia, and the Pacific."

"Terrific, but I'm looking for my brother."

"We carry a multinational crew of five hundred volunteers whose service is a practical expression of their faith."

"That's great, but—"

"Whatever you're looking for," added a taller guy from the back, "we can help you find it. Just click on one of the tour destinations on the menu."

There was a swooshing noise, and a banner appeared as if painted in the air.

"Click here for Administration." The guide pointed to the top of the list. "Here for Book Exhibition. Here for the Deck Department."

"Have you seen a boy about my age, kinda looks like me but with rounder cheeks and glasses, sand in his hair? He'd be chasing a beagle."

"Click here for Engine Department." The guide kept pointing the way he'd been programmed to. "Here for Steward Department. Here for Events and Functions."

Ashley sighed. Making these Web people understand her was going to be a little harder than she'd expected. At least there wasn't any double-clicking going on…yet.

"What's the Steward Department?" she wondered aloud.

"Ah, very good." He touched a knife-and-fork icon, and Ashley held her breath, waiting for the electric tingle—which didn't come. Maybe it only happened between sites and not when she jumped between different parts of the same site.

When she opened her eyes, she was standing in a long, narrow kitchen with a grill along one side and a counter along the other. A smiling cook dressed in a white apron was flipping several dozen burgers.

"Oh!" The cook straightened up, spatula in hand. "Welcome to the galley. The galley on board a ship is the place where all the food is prepared, and here that means, on average, more than one thousand meals a day. On the *Logos II* we have…"

Ashley listened to her new Web guide as she looked around the kitchen—er, galley. "Seen any dogs lately?" she finally interrupted.

The cook gave her a puzzled look, as if to say, "No dogs on this menu."

"Meals are prepared to please the taste buds of Asians, Europeans, Africans, and Americans while maintaining a balanced diet…"

"Thanks anyway."

Time to get out of here. Ashley touched the menu to visit the Engine Department (loud), the Deck Department (aye, aye, Captain), the Communications Department (hello), and finally the Book Exhibit Department.

"This is terrible!" A woman stood next to a stack of books on the rear deck, waving a shredded book in her hand. "Just terrible. Did you see where that internaut with the dog went after it chewed this?"

She wasn't talking to Ashley but to another worker who was helping clean up the mess.

"And our Bibles! I don't think the dog had anything to do with those, but now all of them are gone!"

"Excuse me." Ashley stepped up. She didn't know any-thing about missing Bibles, but... "Did you say dog?"

"Oh!" A helpful Web-guide smile appeared on the woman's face. "Welcome to the Book Display deck. This is our store. We carry a stock of half a million books covering a wide range of subjects, such as science, technology, sports, hobbies, cookery, the arts, and...well, naturally we used to carry Bibles, but something seems to have happened to them. These books are chosen—"

"That book you're holding." Ashley meant the chewed one the woman was now holding behind her back. "Did a beagle do that?"

"Beagles and budgies!" cried the woman. "Books about animals. Aisle three, table twenty-two."

"No, you don't understand my question."

Uh-oh, she'd said the magic word. Sure enough, here came Mr. FAQ, looking dapper in his black-and-white tux. How did he keep it so clean, zipping around the Internet?

"Does someone have a question?" he asked. "I'm here to answer your most Frequently Asked Questions. Something about beagles, was it?"

"My aunt's beagle. I'm—"

"Ants? You must mean hymenopterous insects of the Formicidae family that live together in highly organized colonies, including wingless workers and a single queen. There are many varieties living worldwide. Please ask me another FAQ."

"No, no, no. I'm talking about *my* aunt."

"Mayan? The Mayans built a major civilization sometime between 300 BC and AD 900 in the area that is now known as Mexico, Guatemala, Honduras, and Belize."

"Belize? Puh-lease! I said aunt! As in my mom's sister. And the name of the beagle I'm looking for is Applet. I just wanted to know if—"

"Ah yes. An applet is a small computer program designed to perform a specific job. It's often used for animations or calculations and can be sent along with a Web page to a viewer.

Would you like to know anything about object-oriented programming languages?"

Object-WHAT? Ashley closed her eyes and tried not to scream. No offense, but this Mr. FAQ was pretty useless.

"Just get me off this wreck," she muttered to herself.

"Ah, wrecks!" Of course, Mr. FAQ seemed to know something about those, too. "Your internaut friend wanted to know about those as well."

Ashley's ears perked up as he went on.

"On January 4, 1988, the original *Logos* ship was lost on a reef off the coast of Chile. For a more complete description of the tragedy, click here."

Aha! *The Sinking of the Logos* link! Yet another famous shipwreck.

"Where?" Ashley stepped closer to see where the cyber-butler was pointing.

Actually, a little too close.

HOUSTON, We've HAD A
PROBLEM

Whoops! Austin ducked his head so as not to bump the control panel, but instead he drifted sideways and brushed against a row of switches.

He squinted to see better in the dark, damp chill. *Brrr.* All of a sudden his stomach didn't feel too wonderful. He'd always thought being weightless would be more fun than this.

Good thing a little sunlight made it through the tiny round windows of this tin can of a spacecraft, which felt something like the pilot's compartment of a jet airliner. With all the lights dimmed, Austin could barely make out three shadowy men strapped to their seats. They were so still... Were they even alive?

The men wore light-colored coveralls and looked as if they hadn't shaved in days. They reminded Austin of how scrunched up in the corner of the backseat Ashley had been last summer on their way home from Montana. She never had found space to stretch out her long legs.

Finally, the man closest to Austin moved to punch a few numbers into a calculator and write something on a floating clipboard.

"Anybody home?" Austin's breath fogged in front of his face. Was this what it was like to be inside a refrigerator? The walls dripped. The windows were all wet. And it smelled like a locker room. He plugged his nose and tried not to breathe.

"Not exactly the *Starship Enterprise,* huh?" The man barely looked up from his clipboard, as if it would hurt him to move.

"I guess not. Is this a shipwreck site?" Austin couldn't stop shivering. "I thought I linked to a shipwreck site."

"Shipwreck?" The astronaut flashed a weak smile at him, though he talked barely above a whisper. "Yeah, you might call it that. This is a ship and we're wrecked. Only this shipwreck is about two hundred thousand miles from Earth. Welcome to *Apollo 13.*"

"No kidding?" At least now Austin knew where he was. "I saw a movie about your story once. Tom Hanks was in it. Part of your spaceship blows up so you can't land on the moon, and you don't know if you can make it back home."

The astronaut nodded.

"This is a NASA site. I don't know anything about any Tom Hanks, but the rest sounds about right."

"He's an actor. You guys make it home okay, don't you?"

"Hey!" The astronaut's face clouded over as he held up a warning finger. "That's on another part of the Web site."

"Sorry. Maybe that's where my sister went. I was right behind her."

The man's face softened as if Austin had just told a joke.

"Why didn't you say so?" He chuckled and waved his hand at the inside of the tiny space capsule. "That's a good one. Looking for your sister on *www-dot-apollo13disaster-dot-com*."

Austin tried to laugh along but didn't do very well.

The man let his clipboard drift. "Yeah, well, no sisters here, kid. Just three cold, tired astronauts trying to get home in one piece." He sighed and put out his hand. "Fred Haise, by the way. I'm the lunar module pilot, and I'm on watch for now."

Austin made sure he kept his left hand behind his back. No use creeping anyone out at the sight of his see-through fingers. He offered his right hand. Shaking Haise's hand gave Austin a tingling feeling.

"You know, I hate to bother you. I mean, I can tell you're really busy and everything, but you haven't seen a dog either, have you?"

"A dog?" Haise's eyes lighted up. "Now *that* I can help you with."

"No kidding?"

Without another word, the astronaut brought two fingers to his mouth and whistled loudly enough to be heard all the way back home in Normal. If the other astronauts in the capsule had been asleep before, they weren't now.

The whistle hadn't stopped echoing in poor Austin's ears before he was staring eye to eye into a large, shaggy face. Actually, white fur covered where the eyes must have been, just as it did on any other English sheepdog.

If you could call this six-foot mountain of fur an English sheepdog. It was more like an English sheep elephant. He came complete with a sturdy leash hanging from his collar and breath that could wilt flowers at twenty paces.

Austin gasped and covered his mouth and nose.

"This is Fetch," announced Astronaut Haise. "He's a search engine."

"Fred!" Obviously, the other astronauts were awake by now. "Good grief. Not the dog again! Get this thing off my lap, would you?"

Haise ignored his companions, grabbed the end of the dog's leash, and held it out to Austin.

"You were looking for a dog, right?"

"Well…"

"Just hold on to the leash. Fetch will search for your sister."

Austin hesitated, but the astronaut held the leash out to him.

"Go ahead."

"What will he do when he finds her? Is he hungry?"

"No, no. Just hold on. If I were you, I would not lose track of your new canine friend."

Austin nodded and took the leash at last. After wishing the astronauts well, he did as he was told. He told Fetch whom he was looking for and held on.

"No problem," he said. "This is just like—"

Just like water-skiing behind a 747.

"Heeeey!"

Austin didn't know how to yell any louder. He was hoarse after already flying through a dozen Web sites.

"Can we take a break?" he asked, his head spinning. Fetch the search engine didn't answer. He kept doing what he does at every site:

Flies in with Austin at the end of his leash. (Austin's feet never touch the ground.)

Stops. (That *thud* is the sound of Austin hitting Fetch's back.)

Sniffs.

Ashley? Applet?

Shakes his big, furry head.

Then takes off once more with the leash (and Austin) dragging behind.

"Here we go agaaaaaaain!"

They crashed into *Weird & Useless Facts About the* Titanic, where a man sitting behind a desk piled high with papers told them how the famous ship's fourth smokestack was built just for looks.

But they found no Ashley at *www.Weird&Useless.com,* and no Applet either. "No sign of them." "Haven't heard of them, sorry." "Have you tried *www-dot-TitanicDisaster-dot-com?*" people asked.

"WOMEN AND CHILDREN FIRST!"

An older gentleman with a megaphone and a dark blue sea captain's hat hollered at them as they rushed through the next site. Had the captain seen Ashley or Applet?

"NO, I HAVE NOT. NOW MOVE TO THE REAR OF THE LIFEBOAT IMMEDIATELY!"

By this time Austin could see that at least Fetch was following some kind of pattern. *Titanic.* Sea disasters. Shipwrecks. At this rate they would have all 250 gazillion sites on the World Wide Web searched in about, say, forty-seven years.

"Hey, let me know if we're going underwater again, will

you?" Austin sputtered and pulled a baby squid off his ear as they heard the deep voice of an offscreen announcer.

"And if you enjoyed this classic adventure, you'll also love..."

Strange how so many of the sites had something to sell—"available on DVD for a special low introductory price for our valued Internet customers." Suddenly Fetch stopped a few extra moments to sniff one of the links more closely.

"What's up?" Austin moved closer to see. "Did you find—"

He didn't get to finish his question before Fetch jerked the leash and dragged him straight through the *Buy It Now* link.

CHAPTER 9

Lost in Cyberspace

Ashley snuggled underneath the warm, knit-wool blanket she'd been given by one of the ship's crew members. Was this the third ship she'd been on? This one might have been perfect if not for the fact that

a. she was still lost deep inside the Internet,

b. she had no idea how to get home,

c. Austin had disappeared into another shipwreck link, and

d. Applet was probably chewing her way into even more trouble.

See? Perfect. Just a few teensy details to fix, like the pitching deck below her feet that wouldn't stay still for anything. Or the pale faces of the people all around her, even that of the serious-looking young man in the junior officer's cap. He wrestled the ship's large, spoked steering wheel as he stared at the darkened view ahead. A faint red glow from inside a brass compass made his cheeks look pink.

Where's Jessi when you need her? Not that Ashley's aunt could do anything about this nightmare.

Could she?

Either way, Ashley was out of here as soon as she could find a link that said *Normal, Illinois.* She tried to see where they were going, tried to peer through the forward-facing, salt-stained windows. No good. All she could make out were the shadows of water and waves all around them. Still the ship pushed ahead.

"Has anybody here ever heard of the *Titanic*?" she wondered aloud. "You're linked to that site, you know."

Maybe the people around her couldn't hear what she said over the howling of the wind and the beating of the waves. Wasn't this the *Logos*? And didn't it hit a reef off the coast of Chile on January 4, 1988?

Off in the corner, a group of three deck hands gripped one another by the shoulders and bowed their heads. She heard bits and pieces, enough to tell they were praying. Yes, agreed Ashley, this was probably a good time to pray, but she didn't join in.

I already know what's going to happen, she thought.

"And besides," she reminded herself aloud so that it would stick and she would remember, "this isn't real anyway."

"It's real enough."

"Oh!" Ashley looked up to see the woman from the *Titanic*—the one with the long, straight, black hair and the purple and pink flowered blouse.

"I didn't mean to startle you," she told Ashley with a smile.

"No problem." Ashley got her breath back. "I'm fine."

"Ms. Mattie Blankenskrean." The woman held out her hand. "Sorry I had to hurry off the *Titanic* before we could be properly introduced. I had a few more sites to visit."

Ashley stared at the woman's hand for a moment.

"It's okay," said Ms. Blankenskrean. "I'm real. Can't you tell we're clearer than the others? Better resolution."

Ashley took the hand, and it felt as warm as her mother's. "So you're an internaut?"

Finally, another human being!

Ms. Blankenskrean laughed, and it seemed strangely out of place. "That's what they call us Outsiders. Actually, I'm a Webmaster. I fix sites that aren't working, er, quite properly."

"That's great!" Ashley felt relieved. "Can you get me back to Normal? I mean, Normal, Illinois?"

"You don't need to explain, dear. That's where I'm from too. We came in through the same network."

Whatever that meant.

"But can you help me find my brother? And our aunt's beagle? They're in here somewhere too."

"Patience, dear. First I need to make a few more adjustments to this site."

"Adjustments?"

The woman nodded at the three praying crew members and pulled her PDA from a large pocket in her skirt.

"Over there, see?" She touched a couple of buttons on the handheld. The trio raised their heads with questioning looks on their faces before fading completely.

"There. It's all very simple, very minor." She smiled and replaced the PDA in her pocket. "I'm just cleaning things up a bit. Routine maintenance for the Normal Council on Civil Correctness."

"But where did they go? Weren't they just praying?" Ashley was confused.

"Praying? Oh no, I don't think so."

"But they were. I heard them."

For a moment the woman's eyes hardened, then she smiled again.

"Well, dear, in any case you don't need to concern yourself about it."

Ashley still wasn't sure what to make of what she'd just seen, but here was the woman who held her ticket home. Best not to ask too many questions.

"I'll tell you what." This woman's smile never left her face. "I have one more assignment to take care of. In the meantime, why don't you just make yourself comfortable here and wait."

"You'll be back?"

"Naturally. We internauts have to stick together, don't we? I assume you wouldn't want to be lost here on the wreck of the *Logos* forever."

"This is another wreck, then."

The woman brushed a stray hair from her forehead.

"A pity, don't you think? All these shipwrecks. If people would only learn to rely on themselves a bit more, we'd have much less trouble in this world. Don't you agree?"

The woman's dark eyes locked on Ashley's. For a moment Ashley thought she knew what a hamster felt like when faced down by a hawk. The hair on the back of her neck stood up.

"Uh…"

No, Ashley didn't agree. But for once her lips wouldn't move quickly enough. Mattie Blankenskrean didn't seem like the kind of person you argued with.

"Good." The woman nodded. "Now, remember, don't move. If you do, I may not be able to find you again. And don't speak with anyone on the site. They're still under adjustment, and you wouldn't want to spoil the site's programming, would you?"

"No, I guess not." Ashley shook her head weakly as the woman went on.

"I'll be back in just a little while to help you and your brother. And your dog."

She retrieved her PDA and touched a corner of the screen.

"Now, where was that link...?" She swiveled when a panel by the floor lighted up. "Ah yes. *Ancient Sea Disasters*. Ta-ta."

A second later she faded away to her next assignment, leaving Ashley clinging to her blanket. The ship seemed to shudder when it sliced through yet another wave.

So did Ashley, but for a different reason. The dark clouds outside looked darker than ever.

CHAPTER 10

Buy It Now

There was no question in Austin's mind why the link was called *Buy It Now*. This time Fetch came in handy as a shield from an army of guys in white shirts and bright red ties. And the canine shield worked pretty well—until the men started streaming around both sides of the big animal.

Charge!

"We guarantee full satisfaction, or double your money back!" said one of the sales army. "All we need is your credit-card number here."

"I don't have a credit card." Austin looked for an escape.

"Did somebody say he needs a credit card?" Another guy slid around from Fetch's back end.

"Do I have a deal for you!" Yet another salesman followed. "All you do is sign here for our free offer, and we promise we'll bother you for the rest of your life!"

"Thanks, but I'll pass." Austin grabbed a handful of white shaggy fur and hoisted himself up on Fetch's wide back.

"Our rates are lower than his!" A man hurried toward him from the front. "Zero percent for the first thirty days."

"Sounds impressive, but—" Austin wasn't sure how polite he needed to be to a virtual salesman. After all, the guy wasn't real.

Fetch didn't seem interested in sticking around either, since he was onto a scent. Austin had to hold on with both hands to keep from flipping forward. The *Buy It Now* link led them to an offer for the *In Search of the Castaways* DVD (another shipwreck?), which led them to a smiling photo of an actress named Hayley Mills (who was in the Disney version of that movie), which led them to a long menu of names such as Mel Gibson, Meryl Streep, and Arnold Schwarzenegger. The names blinked across a neon sign that looked like it could have been lifted off the outside of the Normal Theater.

"Movie actors?" Austin held back as Fetch gave the flashy menu a good, long sniff. "What does this have to do with my sister or Applet?"

Fetch gave Austin an over-the-shoulder glance, as if to say, "Trust me. The nose knows!" By this time Austin knew enough to hang on as they leaped through to the next link.

China?

The building, with its steep, jade green roof and curly corners, told Austin it might have been. But a second look told him that despite the fancy Chinese building, they weren't exactly in Beijing.

"Look at all these people." Most had cameras around their necks, and all of them were crowding around something on the sidewalk. Actually, the sidewalk looked more like a patio or plaza in front of the grand building. "What is this place?"

Austin wasn't expecting an answer from the silent Fetch. He also wasn't expecting a smiling cyberbutler to pop up in front of him.

Mr. FAQ! "Have you seen Ashley anywhere?"

"I'm so very pleased you asked," the man told him. "But let me answer your first question first."

And without any other invitation, he went on to explain all about Mann's Chinese Theater in downtown Hollywood, California. It was perhaps the most famous theater in the world, he said. And this site could take him on a grand tour. The setting for grand movie premieres, Mann's was where *Star Wars* fans had camped out for over a month to see the newest film. And it was also the home of the famous Forecourt of the Stars, where dozens of movie stars had left their hand prints in the sidewalk. (And three famous horses had even left their hoof prints!)

"That's all real interesting," Austin said from his perch, "but what about Ashley and Applet?"

"Ah, your sister and the beagle. I did have a pleasant exchange with Miss Ashley before she departed to another link—I believe it was to a shipwreck. The dog was not in her company. However, I would be glad to tell you more about beagles, which as a breed can be traced back to ancient Greece and Rome. In fact…"

Austin groaned. Even Fetch didn't seem to be listening. He stiffened like a hunting dog pointing at a duck.

Not at Donald Duck, whose famous webbed foot had been set in a block of cement right below their feet.

"What's up, boy?" Austin tried to make out what the furry search engine had seen, but the crowd had become too thick. Add to that the growing number of double-clicking hand icons drifting down from above, and it was time to take a closer look. Leash in hand, Austin slipped off to poke around just as the crowd started shouting.

"Oh!" said about fifty people at the same time.

"Stop it!"

"Over there!"

"No, over here!"

The crowd just ahead of Austin did a Moses-parting-the-Red-Sea move, where half the people split off to the left and half split off to the right. Through the middle came a beagle with wet cement all over her paws and a wide-eyed expression on her face as she zigged and zagged through the gap like a badly hit ball on a bumpy pool table.

"Applet!" Austin hollered, but the crowd closed up as quickly as it had parted.

Bless his little search-engine heart, good old Fetch must have decided he wasn't going to let this chance pass him by. He'd found what he was looking for. Austin managed to hold on as Fetch once more led the charge, and together they bulldozed a hole through the crowd.

"Gangway!" yelled Austin, in case anyone heard or cared. Whether they chose to or not, people made way for Fetch.

Ahead, two security guards were helping a sputtering movie starlet in a silver-sequined dress get up from the wet cement.

I thought she was only supposed to put her hands in the stuff, thought Austin, taking in her cement-caked dress. Still, he didn't think Applet's paw prints in the cement looked so bad. And with the way the shouting people were closing in, he could see the beagle really didn't have any choice but to head back the way she'd come.

"Aaah-EEEE!" Maybe the young woman was a famous singer, too. She definitely had the lungs for it as the beagle knocked her off her high-heeled feet—back into the cement.

It would probably take awhile to clean the wet cement from her hair. Austin would have felt bad for her if it hadn't looked so funny.

He'd have to laugh about it later, though. One of her bodyguards took a swipe at Applet as she zipped past.

Bad idea. When he missed, he lost his balance and added his own full-body imprint next to the diva's.

Fetch almost managed to reach the escaping beagle before she backtracked through the mess. Almost. As the search engine made a flying leap, Austin gripped the end of Fetch's leash with one hand and leaned down to scoop with the other hand. He'd seen Indiana Jones do something like this once.

"Gotcha!" Mission accomplished!

Nabbed as if by helicopter rescue, Applet squirmed but started licking Austin's cheek after she was plucked from the ground.

"No time for that now, girl." With the added weight of a cement-crusted beagle, Austin knew he wouldn't be able to hold on to the speeding search engine much longer.

"Fetch?" He looked up at the mass of fur that covered the sheepdog's face. "Now would be a good time for another link. Quick!"

CHAPTER 11

Hunt-and-Peck

"I give up." Jessica clicked on the button next to the laptop's trackpad until she thought it would break. "Where did you guys go anyway?"

After an hour of searching on Austin's rebooted computer in the Websters' dusty old garage, Jessie felt her eyes going buggy. Sure, she'd powered the machine back up okay, but searching for her missing niece and nephew—and Applet— wasn't anything like online shopping. This was no fun.

Neither was listening to that *Gilligan's Island* theme music as it played over and over and over. She tried to switch off the sound but couldn't. For a break, she clicked over to a few of her online favorites, a site for Christian girls and a couple of fashion sites. No sign of anybody there.

But hey, they had to give her credit. For a while she'd been just one step behind them, although from the *Titanic* site, she'd temporarily gotten a little sidetracked on the *Leonardo*

DiCaprio links. But she'd somehow managed to catch up to them on *Gilligan's Island;* it wasn't her fault Austin and Ashley had hidden in the bushes when she'd tried clicking on them. Instead of hiding, they ought to have come out and thanked her for trying to rescue them.

Of course, even if they had, what could she have done? Reach into the laptop and yank them out? This was too weird. She tried a *Question-and-Answer* site to see if she could get some ideas, but so far that was getting her nowhere. She clicked on the Ask-Me-Here icon for answers to all kinds of problems or questions.

"What do I do," she typed into the blank, "if my friends have been sucked into the Internet?"

Searching, said a box with a picture of a smiling man in a black tuxedo. He looked like some kind of butler. "Please wait."

Jessi chewed her peppermint sugarless gum and wondered what she would tell her sister and Mr. Webster if Austin and Ashley didn't come home soon. And Applet! What about the dog show?

Do you want me to tell you about friends? came the butler's first reply.

My freinds? she typed back. *Whoops,* she thought.

Remember, i *before* e *except after* c, *or*—replied the butler.

Friends. Jessi spelled it the right way this time. *Lost.*

Losing friends can be a difficult part of growing up. The butler had an answer for this. *Sometimes when we move, we have
to make new friends. Would you like to learn more about building relationships?*

"Ack, no!"

Jessica mussed her blond mop, scratching her head and
trying to think of another way.

"Maybe I should try a search motor," she mumbled. "Austin is always talking about search motors."

But that didn't quite sound right. *Search motor.* She typed
it in.

Do you mean search engine? came the reply.

"Sure. I knew that." She hit *Yes.*

Four thousand seven hundred thirty-four options came
back. The best search engines. Search engines for scientists.
Search engines for dummies. Search engines for dog lovers—
or at least it had a neat icon with a dog on it.

"That's cool." She clicked on the nice-looking English
sheepdog, Fetch. It wasn't quite as cute as a beagle, but it
would have to do. And the poor pooch needed a bit of a trim
around the eyes. How could he fetch anything with all that fur
covering his face?

Ashley Webster, she typed, then she sighed.

"No way is this going to turn up anything."

She pushed her chair back from the workbench. This

Fetch was useless. Austin's laptop was useless. Everything was useless.

Sorry, she read on her screen. *Fetch did not turn up any results for that search. Please try again.*

Well, what could it hurt? *Austin Webster.* She waited while a coconut spun and spun and spun on the screen. And she was about to hit the Escape key when a site started loading.

Another beach? Or was she back at *Gilligan's Island*? Austin may have been there once, but how long ago was that now? She clicked on a link that said, *Leave a message in the sand for the seven stranded castaways.*

And then she noticed a set of paw prints trailing across the beach.

CHAPTER 12

Backspace

Austin could tell the crowd at the world-famous Mann's Chinese Theater was getting ugly. Well, not *ugly* as in awful to look at. People in Hollywood weren't usually ugly. These people were ugly as in angry. Especially the young star and her two security guards, who had been covered with wet cement as Applet and company came running through.

The good news was that Austin and Fetch had rescued Applet.

And the bad news was that Austin and Fetch had rescued Applet.

At the moment they had two very buff security guards literally on their tails.

"Fetch!" Austin was doing all he could to hang on to the leash and Applet. "Find a link!"

If you've ever seen a playful dog fling a bone into the air for fun, you can imagine what happened next. Not that Austin thought Fetch was being playful. Actually, thanks to all that fur, Austin could never really tell *what* Fetch was being.

But with a *whoosh* the big search engine stopped and flung back his head the way David might have flung his sling when he was fighting Goliath. That sent the leash—and Austin— sailing in a sort of half arc.

"Whoooaaah!" All Austin could do was holler. No matter what, he couldn't let go of Applet. Not after all the grief he'd gone through trying to find her.

Applet's ears flapped in the breeze. Who knows what was going through her beagle brain. For sure she couldn't read the lettering on the button that was getting closer and closer.

But for sure Austin could. Thanks to Fetch, he and Applet were totally Tarzan, flying headfirst for a button that read Back.

Bam!

Austin groaned and rubbed his poor face. Actually, with all the crashing through links and his arm yanking on Fetch's leash, Austin figured a flattened nose probably wouldn't make matters worse. His entire body was already one big bruise.

He stuck out his legs, which cushioned the blow a little. Still, they hit the Back button hard enough to make it click a bunch of times. *Click-click-click-click.* Austin's knees buckled with all the clicking.

Back they went through the lineup of movie actors and the Hayley Mills bio.

Back through the *In Search of the Castaways* DVD offer and the *Buy It Now* sales army.

Back through the sea disasters, the *Titanic* disaster site, and the *Weird & Useless Facts About the* Titanic.

Back through the *Apollo 13* site, and back to *Gilligan's Island*.

"Oh, man." Austin tried to clear the sand from his mouth. "Ha-ha-ha-ha…"

Of course, this Web site had a built-in laugh track and—how could he forget?—the theme song that wouldn't stop. Applet looked up and cocked her head as if she was wondering about the noise.

Austin stretched as he stood. "Nothing we can do about it, girl. Sorry."

Yeah, and those poor passengers were setting sail that day, went the singers, "for a three-hour tour."

Austin checked to make sure his arm was still attached after his own three-hour tour. His left hand was still see-through, but everything else seemed to be in working order. Applet did a spin and splashed playfully in the water while Fetch started sniffing the beach and the plastic jungle.

"Well, we're halfway there." Austin squinted up at the artificial sun as he talked to Fetch. "We found the dog. Now all we need to do is find Ashley."

At least he hadn't been double-clicked by any overly curious Web users. Yet.

"Ouch!" Austin ducked and dived for the bushes when he felt the familiar jab. "Not again!"

This time Applet joined in the fun, barking and yipping each time a white hand came close.

"Watch out, Applet!" Austin called out to the dog from behind a bush. "Over here!"

But Applet was having too much fun chasing the hand—from beach to palm tree, from the lagoon to the washed-up wreck of the *Minnow*, the wooden yacht with the hole in its side.

"Applet!" Austin finally ran out to grab the dog. "I'm not going to lose you again. Come here!"

Too late to avoid trouble now. Applet had snagged a hand icon in her mouth, and she was growling and snarling.

"Let go of that thing!" commanded Austin. Applet only growled louder, and the hand dragged its pointing finger through the sand in a loop. What was it doing?

Had it drawn an *o*? It looked like an *o*. The first *o* was followed by another, then a *k* that was partly wiped out where Applet dragged her paws.

It seemed pretty clear to Austin that somebody on the outside was trying to write in the sand. Austin hadn't ever seen a hand write in the sand by itself before, but considering what he had seen in the past few hours, this was nothing.

o-o-k-u-p...

"If you don't let go of that hand..." Austin grabbed the beagle by the collar and held her back, but she held on to the hand with her teeth.

The hand stopped tracing letters in the sand. *ookupstin?*

Applet flung the icon into the air with a happy growl. It was starting to look like an old chew toy—slobbery and nibbled around the edges. But Austin was too keyed in on the writing to care.

"What does it say?" He paced around the six-foot-high letters. "Ookupstin? I don't get it."

He looked more closely at the scribbles. Could that be an *l* at the beginning? And could those trampled lines have been an *Au* in the middle? "LookupAustin?"

Austin! Who knew his name?

Plink-plink-plink.

He looked up at the sound of someone tapping on a computer screen and felt another hard click on his head.

Everything went blue.

Digital Kidnapping

Ashley held on as the ship dipped and plunged through the waves. Her stomach turned from the strong smells of diesel fuel, coffee, and cold salt water drifting up from belowdecks. No one talked to her as they hurried by in the hallways, and that was fine. The sooner Ms. Blankenskrean came back to take her home, the better.

Slam! The deck below Ashley's feet shuddered as the ship shouldered into yet another wave. How long could they keep going like this? How long could Ashley's *stomach* keep going like this?

"I've got to get some fresh air," she told herself. But hadn't Ms. Blankenskrean told her to wait right there? She found a bulletin board with a prayer-time sign-up sheet, tore off a corner of the paper, and scribbled a note: *Ms. B—Gone up for fresh air. Be right back. Ashley W.*

She tacked up the note right there on the bulletin board.

That should be fine, assuming the woman came back soon to take Ashley home like she'd promised.

Getting upstairs turned out to be harder than Ashley had thought. Was this the way? One narrow hallway led to another, past rows of small doors, past a room full of clattering machinery, past clusters of people who turned away when she tried to say hi. What was wrong with everyone? The boat wasn't sinking yet, was it?

Oh well. She would soon be out of here. Up ahead Ashley could finally make out a stairway. A hand suddenly covered her mouth as several others grasped her shoulders, pushing her to the side.

Ashley was too shocked to scream.

"We're very sorry to have to do this," an older girl with long blond hair whispered in her ear, "but there's no other way."

"Hmmm-mmm-mmm!" With a hand still covering her mouth, Ashley couldn't exactly talk. She was steered into a small sleeping cabin with two single beds, one on each wall. A tiny desk separated the two, and a couple of family photos decorated the wall. The door slammed behind them.

"Her hands!" snapped the leader of her kidnappers, a lanky, college-age guy with dark hair and eyes. "Get her hands before she can erase anything else!"

A second boy grabbed Ashley's wrists and held them together as if to handcuff them.

"Don't hurt her, Blake," warned the girl.

"I'm trying not to," Blake mumbled. But he wasn't about to let Ashley go easily.

"Hey!" Ashley tried to wriggle free, but it was three against one. "What are you doing to me?"

"Check her pockets!" ordered the dark-haired guy. The girl did, then she made Ashley sit on the bed and finally let go of Ashley's hands.

"Where is it?" their dark-haired leader demanded.

"Where is what?" Ashley felt her cheeks steaming. She would have kicked him in the shins if she could have reached. But the girl stepped between them.

"See, Andrew?" She turned to him. "I told you she doesn't have a PDA. She's not erasing anything."

"But she's obviously an internaut!" Blake stood back with his arms crossed. "That makes her just as guilty."

Are they talking about Ms. B? "I don't know what you want with me," Ashley began, "and I don't know what you think this other internaut's guilty of. I'm just—"

"You're saying you don't know the other internaut?" Andrew interrupted. "You were seen talking with her."

"You mean Mattie Blankenskrean? It was the first time I'd met her. She said she was fixing a few things on this Web site and that she would help me get home."

"Fixing! Ha!" Andrew looked at his friends. "See what I

mean? We can't let her get away with zapping every prayer on the ship with that PDA of hers. And if she's doing it here, she could just as easily be doing it everywhere else."

"Wait a minute, wait a minute!" Ashley thought about standing up but changed her mind. "I have no idea what you're talking about."

"Oh, come on," said Blake. "You're telling us you didn't see her reprogram anything?"

"Well, maybe something. I wasn't sure what—"

"And did she erase something that was 'broken' or delete something like a Bible or a hymnbook or a prayer?"

"Uh...well..."

"Now do you understand?"

The boys paced while the girl sat down on the bunk next to Ashley. She said her name was Erin and that she was terribly sorry for kidnapping Ashley the way they had. They only knew that Mattie Blankenskrean had been rewriting their history so no one could ever guess Christian faith had been a part of it. And she had to be stopped before any more of their Web site was changed. "Do you understand now why we tackled you?"

Ashley nodded. If what they were saying about Ms. B was true, then she definitely needed to be stopped. Still... "You could have just come up to me and asked. You know, explained things."

"Blake and Andrew thought you were dangerous. I'm really sorry."

"Yeah, well, so am I. So why don't you stop her?"

The girl shook her head. "We're designed for this site only. We can't go anywhere else, and we're pretty sure she's left our site. But *you* can go anywhere you want. You can stop her by taking the PDA."

"*Take* it? Why?"

"To destroy it. We're pretty sure that's the best way to stop her."

Ashley started to nod when the door burst open without a knock. Their red-faced visitor looked as if he had just run a marathon.

"We just found out that ten more people were erased," he announced. "Ten more than we had thought."

Everyone looked at Ashley, who swallowed hard. This was a lot more serious than finding Applet and her brother.

"All right," she broke the silence at last. "Tell me what you want me to do."

Chapter 14

404: Link Not Found

Austin had seen TV commercials where people had buckets of blue paint poured all over them.

Gross.

In those commercials everybody laughed.

But here nobody did, even though everything was blue, just as if he'd just put on blue-tinted sunglasses.

Bright blue.

Royal blue.

True blue.

"Hello?" he cupped his hands around his mouth and yelled.

No one answered, and his voice dropped as flat as if he were talking into blue Jell-O. Where had Applet gone again? Or...

"Fetch!"

Austin walked around, probably in circles, looking for

clues. A footprint. A trash can. A gum wrapper. Anything. He hopped up and down, hoping to hit a link by accident.

"Yoo-hoo!"

No luck. After a while he lost track of time, wandering, wondering, straining his brain to think of a way out of the blue. At last something blinked just below the floor underneath his feet. Faint, but there it was.

"A link?"

He tapped it with the toe of his tennis shoe. Presto! The blue around him brightened, and a message in big white letters floated up in front of his face.

404: File Not Found. The file was here, and you wasn't. Now you are here, and the file isn't.

Not quite what he was looking for, but his English teacher, Mrs. Sanders, would have loved that one.

At least that explained where he was. Austin had been whooshed into digital blue nothingness. He knew that 404 was the Internet code for Web pages that didn't exist. As in…

"What character is this one, Marge?" Austin could just imagine some guy sitting in front of the computer in his rec room, eating chips and surfing the Internet for *Gilligan's Island* trivia. Maybe he had seen Austin on the beach and said, "I don't recognize this boy. Let's find out which episode he was on."

That could explain why someone might have clicked on Austin. But that was a problem because…

"Because on the Internet, I'm nobody," Austin mumbled. "If someone clicks on me, there's no record of me. I don't exist."

In other words, he had been 404ed. Before he could worry about it, though—*blink!*—another screen appeared, this one with a picture of an upside-down opossum looking very still.

We're sorry, read the screen. *The information you needed was run over while trying to cross the information superhighway.*

Terrific. Another 404 message.

"Isn't there any way out of this crazy 404 place?" he whispered. He backed away from the possum. A sudden *whoosh* came from behind him.

"Whoa!" Austin jumped at the sight of the balding butler in the black tuxedo. "You're back!"

"Pardon the interruption." Mr. FAQ bowed slightly. "I didn't mean to startle you. I'm simply here to answer your Frequently Asked Questions."

"Fantastic!" After all the blue, Austin was glad to see a familiar face, even if it was digital. "What happened to Applet? Where's Fetch? Can you get me back to where they are? What about my sister, Ashley?"

"Just a moment, please." The cyberbutler held up his hand. "One question at a time, beginning with the canines."

Well, *canine* meant dog, and that was a start. Austin followed Mr. FAQ through the blue as the butler explained.

"I'm afraid I've lost more clients in here," he said. "The link you want is..."

Yikes! Before he was expecting to, Austin stepped through the link.

Or rather, he *fell* through. The next thing he knew, a group of people gathered around him as he crawled out from underneath a pile of bird-watching books.

Applet licked him on the face.

"Hey, you!" He rubbed his cheek as he got to his feet.

"Sorry about the mess," he told the crowd. He would have helped pick up the books if he hadn't been in such a rush to find his sister. "I never know how I'm going to travel through a link."

Austin wasn't sure what had happened to Mr. FAQ, but he was happy to see Fetch hovering nearby. He grabbed Applet to be ready when Fetch picked up Ashley's scent.

"Uh, that's okay," a girl told him. "Are you here for a guided tour of the *Logos*? We're a floating bookstore with a crew from countries all over the world. You're standing in the book warehouse, deep in the hold of our ship. Our ship is...uh..."

The tall girl never took her eyes off Fetch, who was knocking over boxes of books as he snuffled around the warehouse room.

"Fetch!" Austin stepped over to grab the end of the leash.

"Is that your…dog?" asked the tour guide.

"Don't worry about the sheepdog. He's just a search engine. Won't hurt anybody. He's helping me look for my sister, Ashley Webster. You haven't seen her anywhere on this ship, have you?"

But by then Fetch had started for the door like a lion loose at the circus, and everyone in the room cleared out ahead of him.

Here we go again!

"Another internaut!" yelled one of the crew as he ran out into the hallway. "And a…*thing!*"

"Hey!" Austin stuck his head out the door and watched the crew member escape around a corner. "What about my sister?"

He didn't need to worry. Fetch was hot on the trail again in an instant, nose to the floor, tail wagging like the crank on a windup toy. Applet wiggled free from Austin's grip and followed Fetch with a beagle "Aah-OOOOO!"

"Wait for me!" Austin sprinted down the hall. "Fetch! Applet!"

But Fetch wasn't slowing down for anything as he bowled over crew members and anyone else in his way. Austin could barely keep up; it was something like chasing a big, eighteen-wheel truck on the interstate between Normal and Chicago.

Applet had the same idea, always staying in the shadow of

the search engine as Fetch led them down narrow hallways, up staircase ladders, through a radio room, past a small meeting room… They looked like dogs in an obstacle-course competition.

"Excuse us!" Austin bumped shoulders with a man in a uniform. "Pardon me."

Odd thing was, nobody seemed to care that a giant sheepdog, a beagle, and an internaut were rushing through the ship. Everyone aboard seemed to have suddenly decided to come out into the hallways. And everybody was either grabbing an orange life jacket or wearing one.

Which could mean only one thing.

"The captain said to abandon ship!" someone yelled down the hall.

BAAA-BAAA! A horn alarm went off in Austin's ear. Fetch seemed to ignore the noise and parked himself outside a door in the middle of a long hallway. Did that mean Austin's sister was here?

"Ashley!" He huffed up from behind and pounded on the door. "You in there?"

The door opened, but the three college-age people on the way out didn't exactly look happy to see them.

"Who are you?" asked a dark-haired guy.

"Watch out, Andrew," warned the boy right behind him. "Another internaut!"

BAAA-BAAA! The alarm kept sounding and people kept hurrying by, squeezing past Fetch.

"Is my sister, Ashley, with you?" asked Austin, but he was afraid he already knew the answer.

"She left for another link," said the girl. "You just missed her."

"The story of my life." Austin hit his head with the palm of his hand. "Where did she go?"

BAAA-BAAA!

"Listen, kid." Andrew tried to slip past Fetch, but no doing. "The ship's hit something, and we've got to get out of here. I wish we had time to explain, but can you get your, uh, dog out of the way?"

"But can't you just tell me where the link is?"

The girl pointed down the hallway to the left. "Two doors down. But please move! We have to hurry!"

The glowing blue letters she'd pointed to said *Shipwrecks in the Bible.*

Fetch moved off to the side and started sniffing at the floor. Aha!

The trio from inside the room didn't hang around to help, though the girl did turn to wave. Austin picked up Applet just as the ship lurched and threw him for a tumble across the floor toward the link.

"Whoa!" Austin rolled forward like a bowling ball. He couldn't say where the cold spray suddenly came from—or the rock that knocked him in the side of the head.

The *BAAA-BAAA* of the ship alarm went silent.

CHAPTER 15

Dr. Luke's Dotcom

Ashley clutched her arms to her chest and shivered in the cold drizzle. The wind off the Mediterranean Sea blew her hair straight back and brought tears to her eyes. It felt as strong as the wind tunnel at the end of a car wash, only without the tunnel and without the cars. Was she really standing on a bluff high above a sandy beach? Strange how wet and wild a Web site could seem.

And how real.

But just then she wasn't worried about the wind or the rain. Instead, she was trying to remember something she'd once heard about...*what is it called again? The Prime something?* On *Star Trek* it was the galactic law that told the crew of the *Starship Enterprise* they couldn't interfere with another culture when they landed on a new planet. That meant they couldn't tell whoever lived there about warp drives or phaser cannons, that sort of thing.

Oh yeah. The Prime Directive. Bet Ms. Blankenskrean's never heard of that.

But as Ashley crouched behind a slick boulder, she knew that like Captain Kirk she had a mission: Find Ms. Blankenskrean and stop her from reprogramming the Internet. Ashley felt like a high-tech spy kid as she searched the crowd of people below for the woman's face.

But where was a pair of handy-dandy, fold-up binoculars when you needed them? She squinted at the beach and the bay. The scene looked just like Dr. Luke had described it in Acts chapters twenty-seven and twenty-eight, a part of the Bible he had helped write. A few hundred yards offshore, what was left of a medium-sized wooden ship had run aground on a sand bar, and the waves had turned the back end of the boat into toothpicks. All that remained were a few feet of the front end and half of the mast.

Closer in, several wooden barrels bobbed in the waves between ship and shore, where crewmen and passengers had crawled out of the water to huddle together in the rain. Five or six Roman soldiers watched over the survivors—all 276 people on board, if she remembered her Bible trivia correctly. A short, somewhat round man with hardly any hair rubbed his eyes and raised his voice as he waved his hand out toward the still boiling sea.

The apostle Paul? She wasn't sure.

If Ashley had known where to look, she could probably have clicked on a menu bar to find out more about the island of Malta and who lived there. She could have clicked on the ship to find out more about how Paul traveled on his three missionary journeys and how he finally reached Rome after the shipwreck. A helpful map might even pop up. That's what this Web site was all about.

At least it was for now.

A faint glow a short way down the beach told her she was not the only visitor to *www.paulsjourneys.net*. That would be Mattie Blankenskrean with her PDA, looking for a way to take God out of this site's story, strip out all the miracles, sponge out all the prayer.

That's what Andrew, Erin, and Blake had told her back on the *Logos* before they had sent her off on this crazy mission to protect truth on the Internet.

"You're the only one who can do this, Ashley," Erin had said just before they'd told her good-bye at the link. "If our guess about this Mattie Blankenskrean is right, it's up to you to stop her."

Well, maybe so. It wouldn't take long now to find out who was telling the truth. Erin and Blake and Andrew...or Ms. Blankenskrean.

But at this site Ashley was going to make sure that no one saw her. Not the shipwrecked people down on the beach. Not the soldiers or the apostle Paul. And especially not the mysterious Ms. Blankenskrean.

While Ms. B made her way slowly down the beach in the direction of the shipwreck, Ashley quietly crawled down the face of a low cliff. She knew it was morning only because the three from the *Logos* had told her so—the sun had buried itself behind the rain clouds that soaked her hair and clothes.

Yikes! Ashley froze after she slid on a patch of loose rock, sending pebbles to the beach below. She held her breath and counted to one hundred, but no one looked her way. From the left, Ms. B continued to slink toward the target.

Down below and away from the waves, most of the men stood stomping and pacing around a pile of smoldering twigs. Ashley wasn't at all sure how they'd gotten a fire started; the smoking wood had to be plenty damp. She crept closer, careful to let Ms. B get there first. Soon she could hear the men's voices.

If this had been *Star Trek,* the people would have been speaking perfect English so everyone out in TV-land would be able to understand them. These voices sounded loud and clear, but the words were in a totally different language. Ashley knew from taking first-year Spanish back home at Chiddix Junior High that she wasn't hearing Spanish. So was it Italian? Greek?

She was glad she had read the book of Acts and could

remember what had happened. Dr. Luke had been careful to write in all the key details.

Somebody shouted again, and Ms. B shrank back into the side of the hill. And for good reason: A mob of people hurried down a trail from the hills above, waving torches in their hands.

Uh-oh. Ashley didn't remember anything about any welcome committees.

CHAPTER 16

Screen Saver

Back home in Normal, this would have been snooping. But here on the Web, it was "research." That sounded much better to Ashley. Besides, she had to find out what Ms. Blankenskrean was doing and saying to the castaways.

If it was anything like what had happened on the *Logos*, Ms. B would sneak up on the action. And then, with the help of her trusty handheld computer, she would erase any signs of faith.

So was anybody praying? *Zap.* That person would hit the digital scrap heap faster than a touch typist could tap the Delete key.

Jesus? He would be a definite no-no. In fact, His name would totally disappear.

Well, how about miracles then? In Ms. B's world, they didn't stand a chance.

Ashley had stayed hidden in the gloom behind the boulders

strewn along the shoreline. When no one was looking, though, she slipped closer. Was Ms. B up to anything else? It didn't matter. Ashley's plan would stay the same: The crew on board the *Logos* had already seen enough. She felt her stomach tighten, and she began to shiver as the cold rain soaked her to the skin.

If I could just get a little closer to the fire, she told herself. Not so anybody could see her, of course, but some heat sure would be nice. A raw breeze kicked up whitecaps out on the ocean.

It was no wonder everybody huddled around the fire. And the welcoming committee had turned out to be just that. Some women in dark shawls had brought baskets of bread for the wet, hungry crowd. Ashley heard her own stomach rumble as the flames roared higher.

A sandwich would be just fine right now, thank you. Extra mustard, please. And hold the mayo.

A tall islander held out his hands and pointed to the rolling hills around them. The shipwrecked crowd seemed to understand his gestures, and people broke off in teams to start collecting firewood. That's when words started scrolling across the barren beach, much like words scroll across the bottom of a cable TV news report while a newscaster is talking about something else. Breaking news at eleven, that kind of thing.

But there was no breaking news here, though the bright red letters came rolling quickly, knee-high, from right to left.

The Web people on this site must have been used to that sort of thing, since they didn't pay the letters any more attention than they did the whistling wind or a small flock of gulls.

Once safely on shore, read the scrolling words, *we found out that the island was called Malta.*

Fine, thought Ashley. *But I already knew that.*

The Bible verses kept coming. *The islanders showed us unusual kindness. They built a fire and welcomed us all because it was raining and cold...*

"You can say that again," she whispered as she edged up behind a clump of bushes. A peekaboo view through the branches told her what she was most afraid to see.

Ms. Blankenskrean was up to something.

The woman had found a cloak to keep her dry, so she blended in at the edge of the crowd. Over the whistling of the wind, Ashley could barely hear her words to a castaway.

"Not to worry," Ms. B told the young man. "Just switching you all over to English so our Internet audience will understand. Making the site more user-friendly. Cleaning things up a bit."

The woman punched a few numbers into her PDA, which no one in the crowd seemed to notice. Of course, most were either warming their hands by the fire or out collecting more firewood. The man flickered twice and started to open his mouth in protest.

But other than Ashley, no one saw him fade from sight with a little *pop-fizzzzz*.

No one except one of the sailors, a rugged-looking man with a wild beard—though maybe he hadn't seen enough to understand, the way he was looking around. As he stepped closer, he narrowed his eyes at Ms. B as if he wasn't sure what he had seen.

"Routine maintenance," she smiled and shrugged. "Nothing serious."

Right. Where had Ashley heard *that* before? She wondered what the first man had done to deserve being zapped. And she wondered how many more Web folks would be reprogrammed or just plain erased if something wasn't done soon.

It all came down to the PDA. "Get the handheld," Erin had told Ashley, "and you can stop her."

Ashley felt her leg muscles cramping as she crouched, ready to spring for the device at just the right moment. A little closer…

By that time people had started coming back from the surrounding hills with armloads of branches, piles of broken bushes, anything that would burn. A few of them were singing. The bonfire sparked and smoked as they threw each load onto the hungry, growing flames. As they did, the words at the bottom of the screen changed.

Paul gathered a pile of brushwood and, as he put it on the fire, a viper, driven out by the heat, fastened itself on his hand.

Well, that hadn't happened yet, but obviously it was about to. The problem was figuring out which of the two hundred–plus people gathering wood and standing around the massive bonfire was Paul. The *apostle* Paul, the one who had written so many New Testament books. Because if Ashley's guess was right, he had no idea he was about to be reprogrammed.

Erased from the Internet Bible.

CHAPTER 17

MiracLe~or Not

🖱

Back home in Normal, taking someone else's PDA would have been called stealing. What would it be called here on the Internet?

Ashley went through the argument in her head one more time. Ms. B was a threat to history. Ms. B was using her PDA to erase important people and truths from the World Wide Web. Ms. B had to be stopped.

It all sounded so logical. But still Ashley held back for another moment until she saw Ms. B approach a group of people who then blinked and faded away.

Pop-fizzzzz.

"Oh, this is so much fun." Ms. B turned away from her latest victims with a chuckle. "Sort of like spring cleaning."

Well, that was enough for Ashley. She couldn't just stay there, hiding behind the rocks.

"Now or never," she whispered. "Do or die."

It had happened before, so Ashley wasn't quite as shocked this time to see the cyberbutler with the dapper black-and-white tuxedo climb out from behind a rock and make a little bow in front of her.

"Mr. FAQ!" she whispered and motioned for him to get down. "I'm glad to see you. But please—"

Of course it was too late to tell him to hide now. Most everyone standing by the nearest bonfire turned to see who had joined them. But that didn't seem to bother Mr. FAQ.

He raised his hand and started to explain in his classy British accent, "I was alerted by several clichés to assist you."

"Clichés?" Ashley wasn't even sure she knew what a cliché was. What did it matter at a time like this? She pulled him back behind the rock. "I thought you were just supposed to answer Frequently Asked Questions."

"Normally, yes." He nodded. "But on the weekends, I have a part-time job as a spell checker. And I'm here to tell you that 'now or never' and 'do or die' are rather worn-out expressions. They've lost their punch. We call them clichés."

"Okay, I won't use them again. How about you help me with some questions then? Like how can I get a hold of that lady's PDA?"

"A good question, one to which I would be quite pleased to respond commencing at eight in the morning on Monday when I will resume my regular duties in the Frequently Asked

Questions Department. Until then, I really must be on my way, unless you have any other spelling or grammar needs."

Oh brother. Mr. FAQ started to step away.

"No, wait! Please stay!" Ashley grabbed for his arm too late. She peeked over the stone. Would she be able to do this alone? Back at the bonfire, Ms. B was still making "adjustments" as a balding man in a worn robe stepped up and dumped a huge load of dead branches on the ground by the fire.

"Ah yes. Paul." Ms. B smiled at him the same way she had once smiled at Ashley. "You're right on time."

"Pardon me?" He squinted at her more closely, as if he had never seen her before. "Do I know you?" He said it in English, since Ms. B had switched everything over from Greek or whatever they'd been speaking before.

She laughed. "Let's just say I'm your fairy godmother. I'm here to update your image. Clean up the mythological mistakes."

Update? Hardly. *Mistakes?* Ashley didn't think so. But she knew from the verse on the beach what was about to happen.

Paul reached down for a few sticks without looking, then yelped and pulled his hand back.

"A viper!" screamed a woman, one of the islanders, and the others gathered around. And though Ashley knew in her head what was supposed to happen next, she couldn't help leaping forward. She couldn't stand and watch a poisonous snake bite someone on the hand and not do anything.

"Hold still!" she cried as Paul swung the snake over his head like a lasso. Yet the viper held on; maybe it couldn't let go. The look on Paul's face told her that perhaps he wasn't enjoying this Bible story.

"I'm all right." He grimaced but held the hand still while the snake squirmed.

"You!" cried Ms. B when she saw Ashley.

Now a new sentence had appeared. *When the islanders saw the snake hanging from his hand, they said to each other...*

"Murderer," whispered a woman. "You must be a murderer! And now you're getting yours!"

The people around her nodded.

Ashley couldn't believe it. "Don't just stand there. Help me get the snake off him!"

But they only shook their heads and backed away. Another woman pointed a crooked finger.

"He escaped the sea, but now he'll be dead in ten minutes. The viper is deadly."

The others murmured their agreement, almost like murmured amens at a prayer meeting.

"It's justice," declared an old man, crossing his arms in judgment. "Fate."

Fate, shmate. Ashley shook her head in disgust and tried to get close enough to grab the snake's head. Did these people really believe that kind of junk? Obviously they couldn't read the verse, which had changed again.

But Paul shook the snake off into the fire and suffered no ill effects.

"Thank you for your concern, young lady." He smiled at her and rubbed the fang marks on the back of his hand. "But I'll be all right."

"Actually, I think the people are right." Ms. B stepped forward and pulled back the shawl that had been covering her head. "They know the snakes on this island. They live here, after all."

Ashley turned to face Ms. B, knowing she had blown her chance to sneak up and grab the handheld.

"In fact, I think we need to clear up the myth surrounding this event," the woman went on. "Because if there really *was* a poisonous snake, then its bite really ought to have been deadly, don't you think?"

"But it says—" Ashley looked down for the scrolling verses to prove what she already knew was going to happen next. But even as she looked, the words began to disappear, the same way they would if someone had hit the Backspace or Delete key.

...and suffered no ill effects.

...and suffered no ill

...and suffered no

...and suffered

...and

"And now what shall we say?" Ms. B looked up from her PDA.

"You're just going to make something up?"

"Don't worry, dear. Death is a natural part of life. We just need to accept that."

"But that's not what happened! Paul didn't die here!"

Paul had quietly sat down on a boulder, gripping his hand. His face had drained of color, his eyes closed.

"Didn't he? It seems logical that he would have if a poisonous snake had bitten him. I think my adjustment will bring the story back into line with reality."

"You can't do this!"

"Ah, my young friend, but I just did. And people will thank me for it. Pretty soon they'll be able to see stories like this on the Internet without all the fables and miracles attached. Just think how many more people will then be able to enjoy the Bible for what it really is."

"Is that why you're doing this?"

The woman's expression hardened for just a moment.

"You have no idea. Now, you're still interested in getting back to your home, aren't you?"

"Not with your help, no."

"Ah, fickle, are we? And after all my effort to return to the *Logos* to find you. I thought you would be grateful."

Grateful wasn't the word Ashley was thinking of. And now she knew she definitely had to stop this woman. She grabbed for the handheld and held on while Ms. B sidestepped her and grabbed Ashley's other arm.

"Now, you listen to me." She twisted Ashley's arm up and backward, and Ashley cried out in pain.

"You're hurting me!" Ashley knew it was obvious.

"And that's nothing compared to…" The woman's voice trailed away as the crowd around them came alive.

"Ohhh, oww! Sorry!" someone shouted from the other side of the bonfire. "Pardon me. Just a bit of a rough landing."

Ashley had never been happier to hear her brother's voice. She heard more quick apologies, then another shout.

"Fetch! You come back here!"

CHAPTER 18

Web Riot

Back home in Normal, this would have been called a riot. As in people screaming and yelling and pushing. As in total chaos.

It was a riot on the Internet, too.

Maybe the people on this site weren't used to visitors. Or maybe they didn't much like internauts suddenly rolling onto the scene without an invitation. Austin rubbed his head and shook off the dizziness as he tried to stand up. *Ouch!* He must have banged his knee on the landing. The cold drizzle hit him in the face. *The things I go through for my sister...*

"Fetch!" he called again, but the search-engine-that-could was hot on Ashley's trail. This time it seemed to lead through a crowd of shouting people wearing old robes, scraggly, wet people huddled around a giant bonfire on a cold, rocky beach. *Not exactly Miami.* A quick glance at the dark waves and splintered boat told him they had hyperlinked to the site of another shipwreck, only this one must have taken place a long time ago.

The good news was that the way Fetch was moving, it looked as if maybe Ashley was here too. Applet squirmed under his arm; it was a wonder she hadn't been scrunched. But Austin couldn't let go of the beagle yet. He knew he had better see what was going on.

"Pardon me." He limped down the path that had cleared behind Fetch. "Excuse me, please. Coming through."

And, surprise, people did step aside for him, but not because he took center stage. The main attraction was clearly over by the bonfire, where Fetch had come upon the mysterious woman from the *Titanic*—and Ashley. Fetch had raised his huge right paw—probably for show—and was looking over his shoulder as if to say, "Found her!" Problem was, Ashley and the woman weren't exactly shaking hands.

"Hey!" Austin wasn't about to let a stranger twist his sister's arm. That was his job. "Leave her alone!"

His voice must have sounded a little firmer and more grown-up than he remembered. The woman looked over at him, gasped, and let go of Ashley's arm. But not before she yanked something out of his sister's hand.

Not bad for an Internet newbie, Austin thought. He'd found Applet and he'd found his sister. (Okay, Fetch had found them.) Now all they had to do was find a way home. And while he wasn't sure what this woman's problem was, well, two out of three wasn't bad.

He glanced around again, trying to find a clue as to where they were. The people looked pretty ragged, as if they'd just survived the shipwreck—except, of course, for the woman from the *Titanic*. She smiled sweetly at him as though she hadn't just been arm wrestling his sister. Maybe she liked shipwreck sites.

Another weird thing, though: While everybody else around them was staring at the show, a short, bald man sat on a rock with his head in his hands, and it looked as if he was praying.

"Austin," croaked his sister, "we've got to do something about this."

She was nodding toward the bald man. And come to think of it, he looked as if he could use a cup of coffee. Or maybe CPR.

"I'm so sorry you won't be able to stay," said the woman, checking her PDA. She punched in a series of numbers, like a phone code, and then looked back up at Ashley. Even from a distance Austin could make out the dark threat.

"Just remember that when you return home, you don't need to worry about trying to find me. In fact, you must never come back here."

"Fine with me." Austin looked up at the leaden clouds, the drizzle in his face. "Come on, Ashley. Let's get out of here."

"But you don't understand." Ashley shook her head, her eyes wide with a look of near panic. "Ms. B's changing—"

The familiar hyperlink tingling and buzzing had already started when Ashley tackled the woman, who fought her off.

What's she doing?!

What happened next was really such a blur that Austin had a hard time remembering the details afterward. He did remember the tingling feeling didn't hurt this time. It felt more like he was in a fog, and everything was in slow motion. As if they couldn't quite get through the link.

So, surprise! When Austin dared to open his eyes, they were still stuck on the beach, the roar of the people in their ears. Ashley and the woman were wrestling for the PDA again, Fetch had disappeared, and Applet had managed to jump out of Austin's grip.

"Wait a minute, girl!" The words echoed in Austin's ears as if his head were in a box. Could anybody hear him?

Maybe not, but at least he could help his sister get what she wanted so badly. He grabbed for the handheld, making it two against one. And the Websters just about had it when a hailstorm of double-clicks rained on their heads.

CHAPTER 19

Back to Normal?

"Ouch!" cried Ms. B, who seemed to be the target of a half-dozen clicks. Austin glanced up from their wrestling match to see his aunt's supersized smile in the distance, just beyond the screen. The cavalry to the rescue!

Well, sort of. Jessi's nose sure looked squashed and funny pressed against the screen.

"It's Jessi!" he shouted, but the words came out weird—kind of the way they would come out if he were trying to talk underwater—and he wasn't quite sure his sister could understand him. Well, right now she didn't need to. But in spite of Jessi's help, Ms. B still would not let go of the PDA, not even when Applet joined the fight. She bit the hem of the woman's skirt, growled, and started to tug.

"Thataway, Applet!" shouted Austin.

For a moment it looked as if things were going their

way—until one of the clicks came down squarely on Ashley's hand. She yelped in pain. "Oww!"

When Ashley lost her grip on the handheld, Austin and Ms. B tumbled backward to the edge of the waves. If they weren't already wet, well...

"Let go of my computer!" the woman screamed at Austin, but of course he wasn't about to give up now. Neither was Applet, and Ashley jumped right back into the wild tug of war too. Meanwhile, Jessi kept up the double-clicking, but they were a moving target of four heads, six arms, and ten legs.

A double-click grazed Austin's cheek. "Watch it, Jessi!" he yelled over his shoulder, but he shouldn't have bothered. A fresh attack of double-clicks pounded them all. *Ouch! Oh!* Their aunt probably meant well, but she had nailed Austin and Ashley at the same time, sending them flying.

But just as suddenly as the fight had started, it was over. They'd lost their prize. The internaut woman sat panting on the gravel, wild-eyed, clutching her precious PDA.

"You had your chance to get home," she panted. "Now I hope you like the weather here because you're going to be staying on this island for a very, very long time."

And they might have if Jessi hadn't chosen that instant to plant a hard double-click on the glass screen of the handheld. Ms. B shrieked as it cracked and flew from her hands.

Only Applet had enough sense to grab it out of the water

before it completely fried. As she did, the buzzing stopped, and Austin slipped the slobbery prize from the beagle's mouth.

"Thanks, girl."

At last he got a look at the tiny computer that had caused so much trouble. A half-broken screen, a few directional keys. One said Back, which of course meant to go back. That sounded like a good thing to do as the crazed woman rushed at him like a mama bear with rabies.

At times like this people often rely on instinct, and for Austin that instinct included memories of every *Star Trek* rerun ever shown on cable TV. And anyone who has ever seen a *Star Trek* rerun knows that if you grab a person who is being hit with a transporter beam, you will be transported to the same place that person goes.

Well, this PDA wasn't exactly a transporter beam, but close enough. Austin did the only thing he could think of. He scooped up Applet once more, grabbed Ashley's hand, and pressed Back.

Twice.

"Give me that, you—" The woman lunged at him.

Austin pushed the button again and again with his see-through left hand. But when a handheld's screen is busted and it has been dipped in salt water (even digital salt water), there's a good chance it won't work.

But still he kept pushing the button as they ran back

through the crowd. The man who had been hunched over and sick looking at the bonfire appeared to have revived in a hurry.

"Paul's okay!" shouted Ashley.

Austin's mouth dropped open as he realized where he must be and who the man was. The apostle Paul!

Even if the Back button had worked to save them though, it wouldn't have changed the fact that the crazy Ms. B was only a few steps behind. Their only chance now was to…

"We've got to find a link!" Austin searched the gravel as they ran alongside the now healthy Paul. Words began scrolling along the horizon.

…*an estate nearby that belonged to Publius, the chief official of the island. He welcomed us to his home and for three days entertained us hospitably.*

"This way!" yelled Paul, and he led them up into the hills toward a low stucco estate, barely visible in the distance. When Austin glanced behind them, the crowd had closed up once more around the bonfire, but he could still hear the woman's screams and threats.

"Let me go, you ungrateful digital disasters. Why, when I get my handheld back, you're all going to be figments of a programmer's imagination. Do you hear me? Gone forever!"

They stopped at the crest of a hill, just below the villa, which overlooked the ocean. Jessi had disappeared, as had

Fetch. At least the drizzle had finally begun to let up, replaced by cheery beams of sunshine peeking through the clouds.

Ashley rested her hands on her knees to catch her breath.

"Well, I hope we've gotten this site back to normal," she panted.

"We'll be fine here." Their new friend smiled and patted Applet on the head. "You internauts should be thinking of getting home."

Nice thought, but there was still one problem.

"I don't know if this thing works too well anymore." Austin held up the shattered PDA. "But if it does—"

"It will." Paul seemed sure of himself. "Believe me, it will."

But in the time it took Paul to say so, Applet had wandered off into the bushes, chasing a bird.

"Hey, Applet!" Austin started after her, then he noticed a faint red glow coming from the hillside. He looked at Ashley and they both groaned.

"Oh no," she sighed, starting with him through the bushes after their aunt's dog.

Another link.

To be continued...

The Hyperlinkz Guide to Safe Surfing

Hey, this is Ashley. I'm going to tell you a little about some of the places and Web sites I visited in the story.

Well, maybe *visited* isn't the right word. That makes it sound as if traveling the Web was my idea in the first place, like we *visited* Wisconsin on our summer vacation. You know we were dragged into this adventure. We wouldn't have gotten sucked into the Internet if it hadn't been for my brother, Austin, and his goofy digital camera.

I'll leave it to Austin to tell you what he saw, even though I think you might like the way I explain things better. He can be a little too high-tech sometimes, if you know what I mean.

First of all, *www.titanic-online.com*. I've gotta warn you: There are a gazillion *Titanic* Web sites. All you need to do is type *Titanic* into any search engine, and you'll find out all kinds of stuff about the world's most famous shipwreck.

Remember, a search engine is a site that helps you find things, kind of like an index in the back of a book. And don't ask me why they call it a search "engine" instead of a search "motor," which is what my aunt Jessi called it. Austin could probably tell you, though.

Back to the *Titanic*. With a search engine, it's not hard to find sites that can take you on a tour of the giant ship. One of the best is at *www.encyclopedia-titanica.org*. There's more *Titanic* stuff there than you probably care to see.

In fact, you could spend days looking up things about the *Titanic*, just like you could probably have spent days wandering around the real ship. When it was built, it was the largest ship in the world, almost as long as three football fields and as tall as an eleven-story building. It had room for more than twenty-five hundred passengers and carried more than one hundred kids. Only five children traveled in the first-class area (in the fanciest rooms with the fanciest food), while twenty-two traveled in second class and eighty in third class. Those in the expensive first-class section could play in the exercise room on the mechanical horses or swim in the pool.

I could go on and on about the *Titanic*, and a lot of people have. But let me just tell you one more thing you might not find out just anywhere. Do you remember that Austin and I heard the ship's orchestra playing hymns while the ship was sinking? That actually happened. But did you know that not one of the orchestra members tried to get on a lifeboat, and none survived? They played songs and hymns for everybody to hear right up to the very end. "Nearer, My God, to Thee" is one that several survivors remembered, though nobody today is quite sure what melody they played to this song. We can be sure the musicians were a brave group of people who did everything they could to encourage others.

In just a bit I'll let Austin take over, but first I want to tell you about a great site, *www.ships.de,* which will introduce you to a very neat group of Christians called Operation Mobilization. OM sends people all around the world in two big ships, the *Doulos* and the *Logos II.*

That's *II,* as in the second *Logos.* The first one wrecked off the coast of Chile on January 4, 1988. You won't actually find a lot about that wreck on the Internet, though the tours of the other two ships are there on the site. Unlike those who sank with the *Titanic,* however, the entire *Logos* crew lived to tell their stories.

Everyone also survived when the apostle Paul's ship wrecked on the shore of the Mediterranean island of Malta. You can read about it in Acts 27 and 28, including all the incredible miracles Ms. B was trying to erase from one of the Web sites about Paul's missionary journeys.

That pretty much covers it, at least for the sites I went to. Oh, except for one more thing: Please be safe when you're online. Actually, my mom and dad wanted me to tell you about this, too. And this is not just a P.S. or a "by the way." This is important stuff.

Think of it as if you're visiting a big city, maybe Chicago or New York. You'd check out the cool tourist attractions with your family. But while there are some fairly safe places, there are also places you might not want to go to at all.

The Internet is just like that. So how can you tell the difference between what's safe and what isn't? Well, for one thing, don't go anywhere alone. That means it's a good idea to check out a filter like the ones reviewed on *www.filterreview.com.* That site will give you all the choices.

Nobody paid me to tell you this. I just thought it was important enough to make sure you know.

So now Austin can tell you anything else he wants. And he probably will!

Hey, Austin T. Webster here. Ashley forgot to tell you some of the most important stuff about the *Titanic.* For example, it carried 1,750 pounds of ice cream and 1,500 gallons of fresh milk, plus 40,000 eggs and 36,000 oranges. That's almost as much as my mom buys when she shops for the family.

She also didn't tell you about the *Apollo 13* Web sites, which give the true story of how those three astronauts made it home after an explosion nearly ended the mission. It's an incredible story, and most of the information online comes from NASA. Let Fetch *(www.dogpile.com)* search for *Apollo 13*—he'll find it for you!

And if you think old 1960s TV sitcoms are funny, there are a bunch of Web sites for those, like the *Gilligan's Island* site. You can find out all you want to know and more. Some of it is pretty silly.

Actually, there's a lot of silly stuff on the Web, and many ways to get lost. I should know. Good thing God is right there for us in the details of our lives, linking everything together. Doesn't the Bible say in Colossians 1:17 that "in him all things hold together"? If you don't believe me, you can look it up yourself. In my Bible it's on page 890; I have no idea what page it's on in yours.

Of course, you can discover a lot about Christians on the Web too, though you sometimes have to dig a little deeper. But discoveries like those are some of the best parts of Ashley's and my whole adventure.

So there you go. Oh, and don't forget that parents and teachers get really excited when a book has some learning value. So if they ask, you can tell them all about the Web sites and the cool facts and the history you read in this book. And all about how my sister and I are stuck on the Internet and still can't get home.

You'll have to read *Fudge Factor* for yourself to find out what happens during the rest of our first trip into cyberspace. But here's one clue: You won't be able to eat the "fudge" in the title.

See ya,

Austin and Ashley

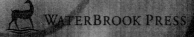

Please visit Robert Elmer's Web site at *www.RobertElmerBooks.com* to learn more about other books he's written or to schedule him to speak to your school or home-school group.